Soup's Uncle

Soup's Uncle

ROBERT NEWTON PECK

Illustrated by Charles Robinson

A Yearling Book

Published by
Dell Publishing
a division of
Bantam Doubleday Dell Publishing Group, Inc.
666 Fifth Avenue
New York, New York 10103

Ellen and Michelle . . .
thanks so much for your help.
Your friend,
Rob

ISBN: 0-440-40308-1

Reprinted by arrangement with Delacorte Press

Printed in the United States of America

July 1990

10 9 8 7 6 5 4 3 2

OPM

Soup's Uncle

One

"I can't wait," said Soup.

"Me too," I told him. "I'm real excited."

"Just think, Rob . . . they're all actual coming, and they'll be here just about any minute."

It was near to dark, and the two of us were lying flat on our stomachs, high on the edge of a barn roof. A perfect spot. Soup and I could possible be the first two people to spot the Hardboilers as they rode into town. Climbing up a long ladder to reach the roof had been Soup's idea. So here we were, daring trouble, perched atop a barn which dangerously stood next door to the home of the town of Learning's toughest and meanest kid.

Janice Riker.

She had a face that would stampede trolls and the breath of a week-old beached oyster.

Fretting about the whereabouts of Janice, whose fist could hit like a bullet, made my neck itch and my hands sweat, so I glanced over my shoulder. Being anywhere within a kilometer of Janice necessitated my becoming more alert than a midnight sentry. Yet I figured for certain I couldn't miss out on witnessing all the Hardboilers roaring into town.

"Last summer," said Soup, "the Hardboilers never even showed up to attend the Blowout."

"The gangs that came were the Sons of Satan, and that all-lady group, the Dusty Angels."

"But this August it'll be better, because Rolly McGraw heard tell that the Hardboilers are the biggest club in all Vermont."

I slapped a mosquito. "Somebody said that another all-lady group would be attending the Beer Belly Blowout," I said, "but I don't guess I can recall their name."

"It's the Leatherettes," said Soup. "And they have earned a reputation of being even tougher than the Hardboilers. In fact, one of the Leatherettes wins the burping contest most every year."

Beyond the mountains to the west, a weary August sun had disappeared to rest, its chores done, deserting an evening sky as purple as old veins or new bruises. My mother had warned me that I should be home by dark. Soup's mother had issued the same order to him.

"I hope they come soon," I said.

Still and all, as the cloak of evening slowly low-
ered, I felt a bit safer. It made hiding from Janice a
lead-pipe cinch. Or so I fervently prayed.

"Ya know," Soup told me, "that my Uncle Vi is
coming to town too. Trouble is, I haven't seen him
since I was a tiny tot, and the pair of us probable
won't recognize each other. Uncle Vi is my mother's brother. That's how come he's my uncle. And
he's also a Hardboiler."

As the barn roof wasn't becoming any softer,
Soup and I sat up enough to ease out some of our
muscle kinks.

"Mama always claims," said Soup, "that Uncle Vi
is the black goat of the family. According to her,
Uncle Vi was a bit on the weird side even when he
was only a kid. He ate coconuts."

"What's so odd about that?" I asked. "A lot of
people eat coconuts."

"Yes," said Soup, "but normal people don't swallow 'em whole."

I giggled. "Is that his real name? Vi?"

Soup nodded. "It's short for Virus."

We waited.

"By the way, old sport," said Soup, "it might be a
smart play *not* to mention the Beer Belly Blowout
to our parents. Maybe we should just ask to attend
some church picnic."

"Right," I said, knowing full well how, in the
past, several of Soup's suggestions had lived to
haunt both of us. The more I thought about it,
however, the more convincing Soup's argument
grew. The term Beer Belly Blowout wouldn't ex-

actly be the sort of event that my straitlaced Aunt Carrie would condone my attending.

All around us, I could see the orange bedroom windows, in houses one by one, clicking to black as the honest burghers of Learning decided to call it a day. Perhaps they didn't know that the Hardboilers were arriving; or, if knowing, they didn't give a hoot.

Soup suddenly pointed.

"Rob, look there. Up the north road."

I looked.

Sure enough, a wee pinpoint of light was flickering about a mile distant. I saw another tiny light, then a third. At the same moment, a faint humming could be heard, coming from a long way off, yet seeming to grow louder, like a wail of ghosts.

"Ah," said Soup, "here they come."

"Wow, the Hardboilers are here at last," I said.

In the distance, there appeared to be about twenty little stars of light, all in a line and moving in our direction. Maybe even thirty. The noise increased its volume and became a subtle yet persistent groan.

"Somewhere out there," Soup said, "is my Uncle Vi. One of those headlights is *his*."

"Which one?" I asked Soup.

"It's probable," he said, "the one that looks dim."

He punched my shoulder. It wasn't anything except friendly, because Soup was my best pal and I was his. Soup's real and righteous name was Luther Wesley Vinson, but everyone here in Learning called him Soup. He was a year and four months older than I was, and several pounds heavier, which was the reason I was grateful for so friendly a punch.

"My mother is always hoping," Soup said, "that her brother, Uncle Virus, will meet what she usual calls *the perfect girl* and then settle down to sensible."

As he spoke, I stopped wondering about Soup's uncle and started remembering a girl I knew locally. Her name was Norma Jean Bissell and I already knew that Norma Jean would always be *the perfect girl* for me. I ached for her worse than a sherbet-filled cavity.

"Yeah," said Soup, "here come the Hardboilers, and my uncle will be among them. My father claims that Uncle Virus is so crazy a nut that a squirrel would eat him, but he sounds like a lot of fun to me. Even my mother admits that, mentally speaking, Uncle Vi is shooting pool without a full rack. All of his balls aren't on the table."

Regardless of whether or not what Soup was saying was true, I was still eager to see all the Hardboiler guys at close range, but I especially wanted to meet Soup's crazy uncle. The rumbling sound grew louder, as all those engines rolled closer and closer. Then, coming around the corner by the gristmill, I saw the very first motorcycle. One by one, a whole line of Hardboilers came into view, with all of their big machines grumbling and sputtering. Slowly they came toward town.

Soup stood up to get a better view of that long line of single headlights.

So did I.

My pal was waving his arms and yelling. "Uncle Virus, here I am, up here. It's *me*, your nephew Luther."

The big guys in their black leather jackets, black boots, black gloves, black hats, and black goggles probable couldn't hear whatever Soup was yelling. Not once did a one of them even look up to notice us. They just went rumbling by in single file, sometimes in twos. I counted about twenty-five motorcycles and riders. The noise became so intense that I almost had to cover my ears. One motorcycle backfired, making a heck of a loud report, BAM, and a number of house lights blinked on again. The backfire caused sparks to fly out of the tailpipe and into the night.

It certain was a sight worth seeing.

It was exciting to know that all these big motorcycle guys had come to our town, to Learning, to attend the annual motorcycle riders picnic, which was called the Beer Belly Blowout. And to ride their machines in races around a track. I couldn't wait to see it all, and I was hoping that my folks would let me go.

"There goes the final one," said Soup.

As the last town-bound motorcycle disappeared around the corner by the big oak tree, I could still hear those powerful engines, but the noise was fading. By this time it was threatening dark and I figured that Soup and I had best consider nosing ourselves toward home.

It was quiet now. Yet I heard a very strange noise. A small noise, a rustle. One that I didn't like.

Soup must have heard it too, because his body twitched a reaction to the sound. "What was that, Rob?"

Quickly I looked in all directions.

Then I saw it . . . or them. I saw a pair of *yellow eyes* staring down at us from the branches of a nearby maple tree. Those two yellow eyes just seemed to be glowing at us from the cover of darkness, hidden behind leaves, eyes that pierced the dark unblinkingly.

"Don't say it," Soup whispered to me.

I didn't have to say a word. We both knew. There was only one evil creature in town that had yellow eyes that burned so brightly in the August night.

The eyes of Janice Riker.

Two

Soup's throat gulped.

"Rob," he whispered, "we're trapped."

"Like a couple of rats," I said, as a cold clammy shudder climbed up and down my backbone as though I were a xylophone.

I looked for the ladder, the one Soup and I had used to mount the roof we were now standing on. No use. Janice had slyly removed it. There it lay, in moonlight, supine on the grass beside the barn about twenty feet below us, totally useless.

"Oh no," I heard Soup say.

Glancing upward into the leaves of the maple tree, I still saw the pair of threatening yellow eyes.

Well, maybe we were in luck. Perhaps it wasn't Janice but only a hungry panther.

My fear of Janice Riker was well founded. In the past she had tied me to a tree and then forced me to chew up and swallow one of my socks. Then, even worse, both of hers. There was no standing up against Janice. Her arm was thicker than my leg and she could charge at you, head down, with all the mercy of an Army tank. Janice was the only kid in town who had spikes on the soles of her sneakers. Built like an ape, but more hairy, she would eat an entire banana in under ten seconds. Janice always won the banana-eating race because the rest of us always peeled ours.

Even when she was an infant, local legend held, the Rikers had trouble controlling Janice. Yet they finally had found a solution. The open top of Janice's crib had to be crisscrossed with barbed wire, and then electrified.

Knowing her, however, had its value . . . like a course in Jungle Survival. At the house where she lived, on the front gate, Mr. and Mrs. Riker had nailed a sign. It warned:

BEWARE

OF THE KID

Needless to say, Soup Vinson and I avoided all direct confrontation with Janice whenever possible, due to the fact that both of us bruised as easily as ripe peaches. Around *her,* everyone else did too.

For me, the hues of summer were usually black and blue . . . the badges of valor with which we all could prove that we'd been captured by Janice, tortured, and then lived to display the sorry evidence.

"She's got something up there," Soup said.

"What is it?"

"Looks to me," he said, "like the burning end of a cigar. Maybe a cigarette. See it?"

"Yeah," I said. "It's a little red speck."

Too late, Soup and I learned what it was. There came a sputtering noise, a hiss, then a small red cherry landed on the barn roof at our feet.

WHA-BBAAMMM.

The noise of the exploding cherry bomb stunned my hearing into a muted silence, mixed with panic, as I wondered when the next cherry bomb would arrive and than explode.

It arrived.

Then it exploded.

GA-BBOOOOMMMMM.

If there was anything I couldn't abide, it was noise. Loud explosions terrified me. Pumping up a football or a bicycle tire took all the courage I could muster, and a small child with a balloon turned me into a jittery nerve. These discomforts, however, were minor indeed compared to the earsplitting presence of cherry bombs. And the fact that the bomb belonged to Janice Riker seemed to heighten my fright level. All the other kids set off their fireworks in July. But not Janice. She waited until August so her victims would be unprepared for her attacking grenades.

"Soup," I said, "I've gotta get down off this roof, and fast. Because I can't take it."

As I ran around the top of the barn, my hands covering my ears, the third cherry bomb arrived. It landed close to where I stood, sputtered briefly, and then appeared to be a dud. There was no explosion. Only a hiss. But as I removed my hands from my ears, there was a sudden detonation that even made my freckles bounce.

WHA-BBBAAAANNNGG.

I could feel my teeth rattling. For several seconds my eyes were crossed and I couldn't speak, as my tonsils seemed to be clanging. My toes felt glued together in a knot.

Then I heard a pleasant motherly-sounding voice. "Janice, dear . . . it's time for bed," chirped Mrs. Riker. "Say good-night to your playmates and then come inside like a nice child."

Janice swore a dirty word.

Her mother, however, didn't happen to hear it as she was benevolently standing the ladder up against the barn. Then she left. Needing no further invitation, Soup and I climbed down the ladder with the speed of which a fireman slides down a brass pole. But from the corner of my eye I'd noticed that Janice was climbing down from the big maple tree even faster. The horrifying possibility of our being cornered, or captured, was still a nagging reality. Knowing old Janice as I did, there was little chance of her trotting obediently home to bed when there was helpless prey nearby. Janice Riker wasn't about to choose sleep over torture.

"Quick," said Soup, "let's hide inside."

"In the hay," I agreed.

Into the old barn we sped, diving headlong into a large mound of hay, and there we stopped breathing. But in only a matter of seconds I heard Janice's familiar pant, a puffing which was warning us of her intentions. If there was any doubt in our minds, it was soon dispelled by Janice Riker's threatening growl.

"I'm gonna get youse two."

As I burrowed deeper underneath a quilt of protective hay, I heard a welcoming voice, that of Mrs. Riker again summoning her daughter to retire.

"Janice, darling . . . it's beddy-bye time. Say good-night to your little friends and come inside. If you're a nice sweet child, Daddy will bring you more cute little mice for your python."

Janice let loose another bad word, and this one was a real ironclad zinger.

But then I heard her hoofs, which I had always imagined were cloven, clumping out of the barn and into the night, heading for home. I pictured Janice curling up in bed, her head resting on a little lace pillow, and cuddling her snake. I had a hunch the python was afraid of her.

Soup was whispering my name.

"Rob."

"I'm over here."

"Where?"

"Under the hay, the same as you."

"Rob, I found something."

"What is it?" I asked, periscoping my head up and out of the hay, yet making sure Janice had really gone.

"Well," said Soup, "it's so dark in here, I can't quite see for certain. But it feels like a canning jar. There's a red rubber lip just under the lid."

As I crawled toward Soup through the loose hay, I said, "You mean the kind that our mothers use to put up vegetables and stuff for winter."

"Yeah . . . exactly." Soup was silent for a breath or two. "Hey, here's another one. And more."

As I groped in the hay, I also found a jar. Wading over to the barn window, I held it up in the moonlight to study its contents.

"What's in yours?" Soup asked.

"*Water.* Or at least that's what it looks like to me. It's liquid, but there's no color to it, so it couldn't be apple cider."

"Mine looks the same way," said Soup. "The doggone lid is on so tight I can't budge it open."

Still waist deep in hay, I moved my foot and felt another jar. And then several more. All of the lids seemed to be on for keeps. None of my jars would open.

"There's more over here, Rob. Lots of 'em."

"They're here too. They're everywhere. Must be near to possible a hundred little jars of water in this barn."

"I know," Soup announced, standing up to brush the hayseeds out of his hair, "that this barn happens to belong to the richest old miser in the town of Learning."

"Right," I said. "Mr. Micah Tightknicker."

Three

"Hurry," said Soup.

Because it was late, the two of us had decided not to run home along the semicircular dirt road, as we usual did.

Instead, we took the Short Cut.

"This'll get us home a lot quicker," I said, panting as I ran, and hoping that it really would. It seldom had.

"It had better," Soup said, "or else our mothers will be reining us in, and we won't be able to attend the Beer Belly Blowout."

"That," I said, trotting along as fast as my legs could pump, "would be a downright shame." I couldn't bear to think of our missing the one cultural event of the summer.

The Short Cut wasn't a road, a street, or a sidewalk. It was merely a very narrow path, up and down little hills and dales, which managed to wind and twist its way from town to where Soup and I lived. His farm was just uproad from mine, which made us next-door neighbors as well as pals. The Short Cut path was lined on both sides by brushy greenery, thorns, and prickly vines. It was just wide enough for skinny kids to run through, but only in single file. Far as I knew, Soup and I were the only living creatures who took the Short Cut, as everyone else wisely used the gravel road.

"Let's stop here," said Soup.

Where we pulled up for a breather there was a tiny spring. A freshet of cooling water bubbled up from the mossy ground, so we each leaned down on the damp rocks, helping ourselves to a long, refreshing drink.

"Rob," said Soup, "we best wash."

Rarely did I ever wash. At a sink I only wiped. So I squinted at my pal in total disbelief. "Wash?" Never did I remotely consider using soap unless ordered to do so by some disapproving adult, usually my mother, Soup's mother, or somebody equally fussy about minor matters such as smudges on the kitchen towel.

Soup was busily rinsing the barn dust off his hands and face. "The way I see it," Soup said as he was scouring his wrists, "a kid has to arrive home either *clean* or *on time*. You can't bust into the house both *late* and *dirty*."

Soup convinced me. I washed. In a way it felt oddly refreshing, and I vowed that I would probable wash again sometime, prior to Christmas.

"Mr. Micah Tightknicker," said Soup, as we started once again to lope through the Short Cut. He was trotting in front and I followed close on his heels.

"What about him?"

"I heard tell," said Soup, "that he's also a little weird in the head, if you know what I mean. His brain machinery is missing a screw. Everybody seems to wonder how old Micah's wallet got so fat."

Maybe Soup was right, I was thinking. Normal people didn't hide jars of water underneath a mound of hay. For some strange reason, I could do my best thinking whenever I was running. At school, I once started to trot around the room during a geography test, until Miss Kelly ordered me back to my bench. Perhaps, I cogitated, there was some strange connection between old Micah Tightknicker's water jars and his reputed wealth.

But I wondered, who would buy water? It was free. We had just used water from a spring without forking over as much as a penny.

"Rob . . ."

"Yeah?"

"We ought to figure out a way to get even with Janice Riker," Soup said over his shoulder as he continued to trot.

"Good," I said. "You could always up and challenge her to a boxing match."

"No thanks," said Soup quickly. "We can't outfight Janice, yet we've always been able to outthink her."

I was tempted to remind Soup that a retarded flea could outsmart Janice, but instead I saved my wind for running. At times, I really prayed that I would grow up to be strong enough and tough enough to handle Janice in a fair fight. Yet that made little or no sense because Janice Riker was rarely known for fighting fair. She was a spitter, a kicker, and a biter. My soft stomach had stopped her hard knee too many times to count.

This meant only one conclusion.

Until or unless I grew up to be a giant, or a gorilla, I would run instead of fight, and it was a lot less painful. Perhaps, I was thinking as I trotted along the Short Cut behind Soup, that when Soup and I attained manhood, we'd become members of the Hardboilers.

"Soup," I said, "let's be Hardboilers someday, and come to town gunning the engines of our motorcycles."

"Sounds okay to me," Soup fired over his shoulder, still trotting. He slowed to a walk, then stopped. "Rob," he said, "maybe we'll be

Hardboilers a lot sooner than you think."

"How'll we do that? We're only kids, Soup, and neither one of us owns a motorcycle. We couldn't even save up enough cereal boxtops to send away for the goggles."

"Rob, old sport, I'm surprised at you. You've never been a quitter."

"No," I said, "and I've never been a Hardboiler either. And I sure won't aim to own a motorcycle that backfires. If there's one holiday I gladly could miss, it's the Fourth of July. Trouble is, Janice extends it into August, the way she did tonight."

"We'll get even," Soup said. "But we'll probable need to come up with some sort of a plan."

"*No,*" I said, facing Soup with my fists on my hips, "*no plan.* Whenever you figure out a plan, it's usual a blueprint for trouble. We're both late getting home tonight, which means we're in Dutch enough."

Soup grinned. "Okay," he said.

Yet I could tell by the joyous expression on Luther Wesley Vinson's face that he already was hatching out some sort of a crazy idea. Soup was smiling. When I think, I run. But whenever Luther Vinson is thinking, there's a leer cracking across Soup's face a foot wide, and his eyes are sparkling like a pair of new dimes.

"Just maybe," said my pal as the two of us walked toward home (late but clean), "we might be able to help my Uncle Vi meet what my mother always calls *the perfect girl.* Then he might settle down here in Learning and teach you and me how to become Hardboilers."

"Well," I sighed with relief, "that makes a mite of sense."

Secretly, I was picturing myself wearing a black leather jacket, black pants, black boots, a black cap and goggles, sitting astride a rumbling engine that was belching smoke and softly backfiring . . . and riding right up to where Norma Jean Bissell would be standing. Her eyes would brighten in rapturous appreciation of my daring and I would win her heart. Then I'd beckon to her with my irresistible black glove, and she'd ride off into the sunset, straddled behind me on my powerful gas-driven steed.

"Yes," I said to Soup, "I might cotton to be a Hardboiler someday. Maybe sometime soon."

"It's all part of my plan, Rob."

"It is?"

"Yep. But remember, get yourself a good night's sleep tonight, on account of tomorrow could pan out to be one of the biggest and most important days in our entire lives."

I stopped. "Tomorrow?"

Soup grinned. "That's right, old top. Tomorrow's a day of surprises. For certain it'll be a treat for me."

"How come?"

We were walking now, and almost to my house. The lights were still on inside and that was a good sign. At least I wasn't going to be lights-out late.

Soup Vinson didn't answer me as promptly as usual, so I repeated my question.

"How come tomorrow's so important?"

"Rob," said Soup, as we parted at my house and he headed uproad to his own, "tomorrow we'll both get a chance to meet my uncle, who is, as you well know, a genuine member of the Hardboilers. Not only that, but he's coming to stay at our house. On his motorcycle. And you'll get a chance to go for a motorcycle ride."

"Wow," I said, "thanks a lot, Soup."

"Yup," he said again, "tomorrow we'll get to meet and know my uncle, Mr. Virus Burdock."

Four

"No," said Mama.

As she said it my heart sank. It fell gurgling into the darkening pit of my stomach, like a pebble dropped into a cistern.

"It's only a little bit after six o'clock in the morning," Mama went on to say, "and I'm sure the Vinsons don't need *you* over there at breakfast time."

"But," I protested, "Soup's uncle is coming today."

Standing at our kitchen sink, Mama's back was to me. Nonetheless, she continued her lecture. "Besides," she said, "you were a tad late getting home last night. So I don't really care if Santa Claus is coming or even Babe Ruth. You're *not* going to plant yourself anywhere near Mabel Vinson's kitchen on an August morning in the middle of canning."

I sighed.

Everything my mother was saying was true. Papa had begun to warn me, weeks and weeks ago, *never* venture into a summertime kitchen where *women are canning.* Several days ago I had made this very mistake, resulting in my being handed an idle paring knife and a bushel of beets. Even worse, I was seated next to Aunt Carrie and recruited under the demanding wing of her close supervision of my laborings. Aunt Carrie's standards of discipline would make a U.S. Marine drill sergeant seem lax.

August, I had also slowly begun to learn, was no time to ask favors of either Mama, Aunt Carrie, or of any other woman in the county. Vermont had two seasons, my mother so often remarked.

Winter and canning.

"Finish your oatmeal," Aunt Carrie directed me. "Then you can lend me a hand shucking those bags of corn."

Sighing once again, I gagged down the oatmeal, drained my milk glass, and started to fake a try for the door.

Turning around, my mother said only one word. "Corn."

It was no use.

There was little chance that I would be allowed to escape to Soup's house this early. Last night I'd been late getting home, and this morning, it had drifted on the tardy side of five o'clock by the time I had gotten to our barn to help out Papa with the first-light milking.

In Vermont, you might be able to rob a bank and get off fancy free. Or perhaps even commit a murder. But to sleep in your bed beyond five o'clock in the morning was a crime for which no punishment could be adequately severe. There was only one worse felony, and that was being late for five o'clock chores in the evening.

Grabbing the first ear of corn, I yanked away the partially dry green husks, and then tossed it into a bucket of its yellow cousins.

"Robert," said Aunt Carrie, "you'll also strip off the silk and remove the runt end."

I did as I was told.

After husking five bags of corn, I was relieved of that task, only to inherit another. My next duty was to help Mama wash out an endless collection of glass mason jars, in order that they might be filled to the brim with cooked corn kernels. Standing at the kitchen sink, I filled a jar with water. Then, just for the heck of it, I added a red rubber canning ring, and locked the lid on tight.

"Look," I said. "This one's ready for storing."

Aunt Carrie squinted in my direction, wiping her brow with the back of a hand which held a slicing knife, and then spoke up. "I don't guess anybody in a right mind would put by *water* for a winter."

As she spoke, I was recalling how Soup and I had been hiding from Janice Riker last evening, beneath the hay in old Mr. Micah Tightknicker's barn.

"Some people might," I said.

"Who?" Mama asked in a toneless voice.

"Well," I said, "you won't believe it, because it'll sound too fooly, but last night, Soup and I maybe discovered a certain somebody who'd save water in a jar." I held it up again. "In a glass canning jar, just exactly like this here one of ours."

"Nonsense," Aunt Carrie muttered.

In the past, Soup had cautioned me repeatedly about my going home and then reporting our adventures to Mama and Aunt Carrie. However, what I was telling these two good ladies certainly seemed harmless enough to me, so I continued with my story.

"Yup," I said, "you dear ladies would be downright surprised to learn that *some folks can water.* And not just in one jar. I mean in lots and lots of them. All over the place." I nodded my head to emphasize my point. Not my pointed head, but the conversational point I was making. "Jar after jar after jar."

A look passed between Mama and Aunt Carrie. It was a hurried glance, one which I didn't quite understand. They didn't speak but only stared at one another.

"Now perhaps," my mother said, "all of this notion was merely your imagination. The excitement of seeing all those motorcycle machines maybe went to your head and then you and Soup started seeing things that didn't really be."

"If you ask me," Aunt Carrie put in, "those motorcycle contraptions are works of the Devil, and I'm not a whit surprised that you saw those dreadful people with all sorts of jars." She snorted. "And all sorts of liquids."

As I kept washing the jars out, I told Mama and Aunt Carrie a bit more about the jars of water Soup and I had found.

"Oh, the Hardboilers didn't bring the jars of water to town. Not at all."

Mama looked surprised. "They didn't?"

"No," I said. "Soup and I were hiding from Janice, and we sort of stumbled into them. By accident."

"Where?"

"At the edge of town."

Mama sighed. "Rob, exactly where?"

"Well," I said, "Soup and I weren't doing anything wrong. Or against the law. All we were doing was hiding in the hay."

"What hay?" My mother's voice climbed a note or two on the scale of curiosity.

My throat began to tighten. In the past, I'd been cautioned to steer clear of Mr. Micah Tightknicker and his property, as the old man had been known to keep a loaded shotgun and took aim at dogs and kids. And at other vermin, skunks, and lawyers.

"Oh," I said, scrubbing a jar really hard until the glass was almost surgically shiny, "just under a pile of hay in some old barn."

Mama faced me. "Whose barn was it?"

"Uh, I didn't actual see the owner of the barn. Maybe nobody owns it." I was lying through my teeth and my mother sensed it. Mama could smell out a lie in a pile of manure. She knew her kid like she knew her kitchen.

Mama scowled. *"Who?"*

"Uh . . . Mr. Tightknicker."

The oatmeal started to rise in my throat. Whenever I wasn't being exactly truthful with my mother, my food often took a notion to reverse itself into an upward gusher.

Mama tapped her foot. "So *that's* where you and Soup found all those old pesky jars of . . . of *water.*"

"Yes'm." I smiled quickly, forcing the rising oatmeal to return to my stomach and hopefully to resume its leisurely digestion. "But we didn't swipe any."

Wiping her hands on her faded gingham apron, Mama took a step toward me. "Robert, I want to know something, and I want your answer straight out honest."

"Yes'm."

"Did you or Soup open any of those . . . those *water jars* ? Did you loosen any of the lids?"

I breathed easier. "No," I said. "We sort of tried to, but those lids were locked on a lot tighter than the way you and Aunt Carrie do, with beets and corn and stuff."

"You must never . . . *never* open up one of those jars," Mama said. "Will you promise me?"

"Sure," I told her. "I promise."

Five

"Hooray," said Soup, "here he comes."

The two of us were standing on the Vinson front porch, looking downroad in the direction of town. The time was exactly noon.

Sure enough, Soup Vinson was right. Approaching in the distance, just ahead of a long puffy snake of gravel dust, was a fast-moving motorcycle, ridden by a rider entirely dressed in black clothes. Louder and louder came the sound of a motorcycle engine being gunned. BAM. It backfired just as it left the road and turned toward Soup's house.

Slipping quickly out of her apron, Soup's mother screamed "Vi!" and ran toward her brother with her arms held high in the air. "Vi," she said happily, "you're here!"

We ran too.

Uncle Virus cut his engine, hooked a long leg off the black saddle, and gave his sister, Soup's mother, a bear hug. Then he picked up Soup as though he were little more than a rag doll, swinging his nephew in a wide circle. He swung me around too. Until I was dizzy.

"Hey," said Uncle Vi in his big booming voice, "it sure is great to be here and see you folks." His breath seemed to be a curious blend of motorcycle grease, garlic, and stale beer.

Never before had I ever met a person in all of Vermont that looked anything like Soup's uncle. Mr. Virus Burdock had a short brushy butch haircut on top, but long flowing hair on the sides. Part of his hair was green. From his left ear dangled a shark's-tooth earring. From his right ear hung a large pair of furry dice. He needed a shave. On the back of his leather jacket silver-stud letters spelled out Uncle Vi's subtle message to the world:

IF YOU MISS YOUR WIFE, SHOOT AGAIN

The leather jacket had no sleeves. Uncle Vi sported a tattoo on his huge bicep, a brilliantly created acrostic of several foul words. Some I knew. Others I wasn't too sure about, except that one or two of them had something to do with a very rough sport. Ice hockey. Underneath the strange words was a bleeding-dagger tattoo, tastefully resplendent in several colors. Yet I thought that Uncle Virus had a fun-loving face, in spite of the railroad-track scar.

Uncle Virus and Soup's mother were talking about how long it had been since his last parole, while Soup and I were moving closer to his uncle's motorcycle. It was a Harley-Davidson hawg, and absolutely the biggest and blackest motorcycle I'd ever seen. A mean machine.

"Wow," said Soup.

In a second or two, the two of us were sitting on the big black saddle of a seat, but our legs were too short to reach the footrests. My feet missed by ten inches and Soup's by six.

"Boy," I said, "it'll be a few more years before you and I'll be riding one of these."

Over his shoulder, Soup shot me a grin.

"Maybe," he said. "And maybe not."

The two grown-ups were looking at us as we sat on the motorcycle, Soup in front, me in back. Uncle Vi was smiling, but not his sister. Mrs. Vinson wore a worried look on her face, one of deepening concern. "Vi," she said to her giant of a brother, "I certain hope and pray you don't plan on taking those two children for a ride on that dreadful thing."

Soup and I cheered the idea.

And I could see by the twinkle in Uncle Vi's eyes

(his goggles were pushed up on his head) that he was intending to do exactly what Mrs. Vinson feared. "Sure I am, Sis," he said. "Can't you see they're both itching for a ride so bad they can't stand it?"

Mrs. Vinson sighed. "Virus Burdock, you'd better go really slow, and be careful. Until you all get back safe and sound, I won't be able to draw a peaceful breath. Now promise me you won't travel at some reckless speed. Please, no more than ten or fifteen miles an hour."

"I promise," Uncle Vi said, turning as he spoke to cross his fingers and throw a wink of rascality to Soup and me. As he smiled, I noticed that Soup's uncle had stainless steel teeth, all of which had been probable buffed by a power sander.

One of the things I liked best about Uncle Virus was the fact that, early on, he didn't want me to call him Mr. Burdock. I'd be allowed to call him Uncle Vi just as Soup did.

"Okay," said Uncle Vi, "here we go, us trio of good old buddies."

Mrs. Vinson appeared to be on the brink of passing out cold. "Vi," she said, "I'm not at all certain that seat is long enough to handle three people . . . especially if one of them's you."

"Aw," he said, "you worry too much. I'll just tell 'em to hang on to me real tight as I take this hot hawg up the ramp and off the edge of the jump into eternity."

Mrs. Vinson's face turned deathly pale.

So did mine.

"Now, then," said Uncle Virus, "how'll we all best fit on this here saddle? Luther, you sit tight behind me. Hear? Robert, you sit forward, right yonder, and straddle the gas tank. Feel okay?"

"Yes," I lied.

"I can't see much back here," Soup complained. "Except for the back of your jacket."

Uncle Vi sighed. "There's only two ways to travel," he told his sister. "Traveling first class . . . or traveling with children." He sighed one more time. "Okay, you sit in front of me, in the middle, with Robert all the way up to the very front."

This worked out a bit more to Soup's liking. And to mine as well.

"Luther, I'll take a purchase onto you, and then you hold on to your pal up yonder. Robert, hold them handlebars with your hands, close to the neck, but don't try to steer or we'll all end up busted. Hear?"

"Yes," I said, "I'll be careful."

"Only a very short ride," said Soup's mother, but nobody seemed to hear her request.

Underneath me, the forward prong of the saddle felt hot and hard, but the metal gas tank felt even hotter and harder. However, I certain wasn't going to gripe. For a long time I'd wanted to ride a mo torcycle, yet never had, and today was my big chance. Things were working out almost exactly as

Soup had predicted. I felt him behind, leaning forward, to whisper something in my ear.

"Rob," he said, "tomorrow we'll go to The Dump."

"What for?" I asked Soup.

"Oh," he said, "you'll soon see. It just might be that my brain is hatching a nifty idea."

As if a motorcycle ride with crazy Uncle Vi wasn't enough to worry about, a second worry was now looming, another one of Luther Wesley Vinson's insane devices. As my knuckles tightened their grip on the motorcycle's handlebars, my hands began to sweat.

"Are you two guys ready?" asked Uncle Vi.

"Ready," said Soup, his voice becoming a pinnacle of fervor. Insanity, I was now concluding, ran in the family.

Swallowing, I allowed that I was also about as ready as I'd ever be.

"Well," said Uncle Vi, "I'm fixing to kick a start into this baby, so grab anything that don't scream and slap ya back." He chuckled. "Here we go, lads. So hang on to your haunches."

The big black Harley Davidson hawg snarled into action and we near to flew out of the driveway. Somewhere, in the distance behind us, Mrs. Vinson was hollering some futile request in a panicky and plaintive voice, one that sounded as though she was suffering, as mothers so love to do.

She probable was.

Once we hit the dirt road, Uncle Vi let out something he called *a suicide clutch*, and the loose gravel scattered out from under us like frightened hail. The engine spat like venom. Uncle Vi hooted out a good old Vermont mountain-man yell, and we near about to took off. Behind, I felt Soup tightening his hold on me, while my fingers knotted around the silver handlebars like vises.

"Hang on," hollered Uncle Vi.

"Hey," yelled Soup, "let's see what this big baby can do on a dirt track."

I saw what it could do.

Just under my chin was the motorcycle's speedometer, and the little red arrow was moving steadily to the right of the dial. Because my eyes were watering, I couldn't read the numbers on its face, but off to the right I recalled seeing 100. And 120.

"Yahoo!" screamed Uncle Virus, in a voice that convinced me that good old Uncle Vi and sanity were total strangers. He was a nut right off a hickory tree. You could grind him up and use the pieces in peanut brittle.

"All this doggone road dust," Uncle Vi shouted, "is fetching me up a thirst."

Without further comment, he flipped open one of his sidesaddle bags, even though we were bouncing along at either an out-of-control speed or close to it, and pulled out a container. Twisting my head around to look, I couldn't believe what I saw. Nor would I ever begin to believe it if I lived to be ninety years old. Tipping back his head, Uncle Vi took a healthy swig of water from a glass container.

It was a canning jar!

"Wow," he said after a swallow, "it's about near time I had me a hard bullet." He laughed a lunatic's laugh.

"Watch the road," I yelled. "Please!"

"Sure thing, kid," he said. "If I don't watch it, sometimes that doggone road up and disappears right out from under my smoking wheels."

We continued on. Even faster. Yet we didn't go through town. Instead, good old Uncle Vi detoured into what was locally known as the Crick Bed Road, down by a slowly moving stream of sludge. Much of its contents was supplied not by fresh mountain springs, but rather by the belching residue of a local paper mill. The crick was more chemicals than water, and once it had even caught fire.

Some of the local millworkers attempt fishing in the wide part of the crick, a place known as Stink Bay. Only in July and August. At other times, the bay is frozen into solid ice, but the ice is usual a surly shade of brown.

It sure was a trashy neighborhood.

As we went by a dump, we screeched to a stop at a place that was even worse. I read the crudely lettered sign over its door, recognizing the infamous name. My mother had warned me, usual about three times a day, that this was a place into which I was *never to set foot.* Soup's mother had issued an identical warning to him. Yet here we were, parking among two dozen other motorcycles, and fixing maybe to venture inside. I shuddered.

Again I read the sign.

SWILL'S HOLE

Six

I couldn't see.

Not once in my entire life had I ever taken a trip away down into a deep coal mine. Yet a mine shaft at midnight couldn't have been any darker than the interior of Swill's Hole.

As I blinked and groped along, following Uncle Vi who oddly seemed to know his way down the stairs, my nostrils cautiously began to inhale the establishment's earthy aroma. It was a blend of sweaty work shirts, stale beer suds, a few bar rags that were commencing to ferment and host fungus, and industrial-strength rat poison. Yet the room smelled better than its patrons.

As the exotic perfume of the place invaded my nasal passages, infecting my sinuses, and then entered my lungs, never to expel but to settle there as sludge, every mouthful of food that I had ever swallowed seemed to be only partly digested and demanding upward mobility. In my throat I tasted the threat of unpopped popcorn, mustard from baseball doubleheaders, half-chewed Milky Ways, teeth-blackening licorice, and at least a gallon of sloshing Orange Crush which was now rapidly curdling.

Oddly enough, there was no conversation.

What I heard as I inched forward into the murk of Swill's Hole, sticking closer to Uncle Vi than gum to a shoe, was a continuous rumbling of deep male voices. Nobody talked. But everyone shouted.

Uncle Vi seemed right at home.

Offering friendly slaps on the back to several of our fellow patrons and barking retorts, Uncle Virus stumbled doggedly forward, bumping tables, spilling a few beverages, ducking an uppercut or two, and ignoring the irate complaints hurled our way in tidy clumps of four letters each. Several of the more colorful expressions I mentally added to my rapidly augmenting vocabulary.

"I can't see," said Soup.

"Me neither," I said. Trying to lift one eyelid, I quickly closed it again, as the air down in Swill's

Hole was stinging and smarting my eyes worse
than a hair washing.

As my vision adjusted to the gloomy fumes and
as we continued to edge our way between tables, I
gradually became aware that very nearby to
where I stood, a band was playing. Squinting, I
could make out some guy blowing "Tea for Two"
through a dented and tarnished Sears Roebuck alto
saxophone. At his side, a bleary-eyed cornetist was
busily valving away at some unidentified waltz
melody that wasn't "Tea for Two." A drummer
banged and thumped with no particular pattern of
rhythm in mind, and a chubby vocalist with trou-
bled skin was singing "Red Sails in the Sunset,"
partly in Italian.

The drummer swung his drumstick at a giant
cymbal, and missed it. He did, however, manage to
strike a seated customer who dully received the
blow and slumped silently to the floor, prompting
his table companions to fight over who would
down his drink.

Nobody down in Swill's Hole seemed to be pay-
ing much attention to the band or to the singer,
even though he was lisping his lyrics through a
bullhorn. Why the vocalist had elected to sing
"Red Thails in the Thunthet" I will never know.

"Rob," I somehow heard Soup saying, "I think
I'm standing on something weird, but I can't figure
out what it is."

Peering downward, and bending low, I discovered what Soup was standing on. It wasn't easy to believe what I saw.

"It's a person," I said. "I can't see for certain, but you seem to be standing on his face. You're not hurting him, though, because I think he's been dead for a while."

Beside me, the band wasn't exactly rendering what anyone would call music. It sounded more like trains crashing. Of its members, the drummer seemed to be the most enthusiastic (or the most sober), as his errant drumstick felled another patron. Looking closer, and much to my surprise, I could see that the drummer wasn't really using a drumstick after all. In self-defense, he was wielding a tire iron.

The three of us again fought our way through the crowd, as Uncle Vi gave me the impression that he was in search of a fistfight. Bumping my nose on a hard object, I stopped, wondering if my nostrils were bleeding. Luckily for me, they weren't. Stretching out an exploratory hand, I discovered what my nose had encountered. It was the edge of a bar. Above the bar hung a sign. Although I had to strain my vision through the smoky darkness, I could read it:

INVEST IN

YOUR COMMUNITY.

BUY A JUDGE.

Lifting my chin, balancing my sneakers on the slime of a brass rail below, I could barely see across the bar's surface, even though my direct vision was obstructed by an array of used drinking glasses, each one cloudy with scum. The bottom of every glass appeared to be encrusted with some brown residue which defied identity.

Looking upward even more, I could finally make out an enormous dirt-smudged apron, above which was a raw round face, larger than a medium pizza. An unlit cigar was inertly lodged in the corner of the man's mouth, as though the cowering cigar butt had found a nook in which to hide from physical harm.

The proprietor glowered down at me, then spoke in a voice that must have spent at least a decade gargling with rusty nails and broken bottles. Or drinking liquids he'd found in puddles on the floor of a garage. "Shorty," he told me, "don't go breathing on them clean glasses. We run a tidy joint."

"Howdy there, Swill," I heard Uncle Virus holler over the din. "These here two little guys are my pals, so maybe you'll pour 'em something to wet their young whistles. Okay?"

Swill growled and grunted a one-word salutation.

"What'llyagonnahave?"

Following his question, Swill pushed the filthiest empty glass of his collection an inch or two closer to where my chin rested on the bar's edge. Before I could answer, Swill's other hand flipped a lid off a canning jar, one which was halfway filled with what looked like water. Without much ceremony or flourish, Swill dumped some of the water into my glass, spilled the rest, and then said a word which was even dirtier than my glass.

He did the same for Uncle Vi and Soup, but in Uncle Vi's glass floated a set of dentures.

Without much hesitation, Uncle Vi hoisted his beverage, holding it on high as though toasting some unseen celestial companion, brought the glass to his lips, and knocked back a healthy swig. After swallowing, it was a full minute, perhaps even a mite longer, before Soup's uncle could speak. When he did, upon gulping down the dentures, Uncle Vi let a whoop loud enough to crack plaster. But then he frowned at Swill, pointed to the canning jar Swill was holding, and complained, "Somebody's been cutting this stuff." He coughed. "It's too smooth."

Swill shrugged. "Don't blame me. I don't do no moonlight farming. Remember, it's still Prohibition, so don't get fussy. This here batch I bought from old Micah."

Soup and I looked at each other. Because right away I figured that Swill was talking about nobody else except Mr. Micah Tightknicker. Looking at his drink, Soup said, "Hey, maybe this stuff *isn't* water."

He took a careful sip.

So did I.

It wasn't really a flavor, but rather more like a burn or a cut. For a moment I was suspecting that my throat had been slashed with a hot knife. Soup certainly had been correct. Whatever it was, it surely wasn't water. Or fit to drink. My tonsils were suddenly smoking. As soon as I could think, hear, and see again, I was aware that Uncle Vi was saying something to Soup and me. In a proud voice, he was introducing us to several friends of his who had suddenly joined us at the bar.

"Boys," said Uncle Vi, "I'd be pleasured if'n you'd meet these here ladies who are members of the Leatherettes."

Ladies?

At first glance, I thought them to be *men*. But then common sense hinted that men couldn't begin to look this rugged. Yet the Leatherettes were models of femininity as they introduced themselves.

We met Dogpound, Man Trap, Disposal, Gear Box, Fistula, Dead Bolt, Blight, Sheet Metal . . . and the twins, Butterball and Gutterball . . . Canker, Flatbed, Natural Gas, Truck Stop, Formica, Spavin, Dimlight, Bane, Dry Rot, Mess Hall, Chicken Liver, Vitriola, Tabasco, Pig Iron, Pickup, Jalapeña, Bedbug, and Pit Bull.

All of the Leatherettes proved to be every bit as charming as their names.

But then something rather important happened. Butterball wanted Uncle Vi to meet their newest member, a lady who had only recently joined their motorcycle club. "Virus," one of the ladies yelled over the noise, "y'oughta meet our new gal. This'n here is Tacky."

From the astounded expression on Uncle Vi's face, I realized that he didn't meet a lady like Tacky every day. Nor could anyone. She had mink eyebrows, one blue eye and one green, pink hair, sequins on her front teeth, a blouse of red cellophane, platform open-toe spike-heel biker's boots, a Naugahyde split skirt (also a split lip), fishnet metallic stockings containing a dead fish, a belt buckle one size below a manhole cover, earrings which were twin mousetraps (one held a dead mouse), and lipstick so thick that it must have been applied by a trowel. Her lipstick was neon and her mouth blinked *on* and *off*.

"Pleasedtomeetcha," said Tacky, her proud but modest pair of nostrils flaring for want of oxygen.

To me, Tacky didn't really look like a person. She appeared to be some sort of a machine. Yet, for some reason, Uncle Vi couldn't speak. All he did was smile, very softly.

And sigh.

Seven

It was the next day.

Soup had somehow convinced me that unless the two of us hustled to a certain location, I would miss my chance to impress Norma Jean Bissell.

So here we were, at The Dump.

Because I was a close pal of Luther Wesley Vinson, he and I visited The Dump with almost a devout regularity. Soup's family, like my own, were dirt farmers. Neither the Vinsons nor the Pecks had an abundance of discretionary income. What little profit our sires reaped from the soil was somehow squandered on the frills and fringes of living . . . such as food, shelter, and clothing. So if either Soup and I needed a necessary piece of equipment, shopping for it in stores was out of the question. Alas, only one reasonable source remained.

The Dump.

It was nicer than any store, for here at The Dump, a kid was free to browse, with no pressure to buy.

To me, it was always a fascinating place, an entire acre of almost functional stuff that people had discarded. These anonymous donors must have been wealthy beyond my dreams, I had concluded, to throw away (for example) a mattress with only one minor imperfection, a hole through which you could throw a barrel.

Here, a baby buggy with three slightly bent wheels. Over there, a tire inner-tube which obviously could have armed dozens of slingshots. These were merely two indications that The Dump was far more than a trash heap. Instead, to our eyes, it was a veritable warehouse of priceless treasure.

All *free.*

"Okay," I said to Soup as I stood atop a mound of rubbish, "why are we here and what are we looking for?"

"Shoes," said Soup.

There he was, below me, shuffling through pile after pile of old clothes, an empty burlap sack thrown casually over his shoulder like the cloak of a poet.

"How come shoes?" I asked.

"Rob, someday you'll appreciate inventive genius. As for today, content yourself with asking only a few useless questions." Soup paused. "Remember, everything I do is usual part of our master plan."

I sighed.

"Soup," I said, "the two of us were doggone lucky yesterday, just to get out of Swill's Hole alive. If our mothers ever learn that we went there, even with Uncle Vi, we wouldn't be allowed out of the house for weeks. Maybe even a month. All of last night I kept dreaming a nightmare that we were back inside that awful place. Swill's Hole makes The Dump look like a church garden. Never again will I go into a place like that or take a drink of that dreadful rotgut."

Soup looked at me. "I thought it was water."

"So did I. It wasn't. In fact, that stuff we sampled tasted worse than toad meat, and I can't believe that anybody would *pay* to drink it. Several times I got up in the night, just to gargle."

"You're lucky," Soup said. "I threw up. While we're on that very subject," said Soup, "we ought to be grateful we didn't *eat* anything there. Swill's chow probable tastes worse than his beverages."

"Gee," I said, "the sign over Swill's bar said European Menu. I wonder what that meant."

"In a joint like Swill's Hole," said Soup, "the term European Menu means their cook is a dishwasher who jumped ship off a Latvian freighter, and swam ashore at Swill's boat dock. Swill threatened to drown him or hire him as a chef."

"Okay," I said, "so here we are at The Dump, and we're looking to find . . . *shoes*?"

"Rob, old sport," said Soup, "the time has come for you to trust me, good buddy. We need shoes. Several pairs."

"What size?"

"Well, any size. Try and locate pairs of shoes that have thick soles, and the thicker the better. If you find only *one* shoe, save it. Somehow I'll be able to balance it all out, or even it up."

Bending over, I sorted through another mound of junk. Who, I was wondering, would want to collect an assortment of old shoes? Nobody, I mused, except Luther Wesley Vinson, author of madness, and an inventor of a series of troublesome disasters. Having old Soup for a friend was about as practical as keeping a bull in your bedroom.

But then I started to think about Uncle Vi. In a quiet little hamlet like Learning, Vermont, the coming of Mr. Virus Burdock was, in my opinion, a breath of fresh air. Or stale air, I recalled, remembering the putrid, unbreathable ozone of Swill's Hole, a place where you could see whatever it was you were breathing. Ah, but nonetheless, Soup's uncle had added an exotic flair to a usual boring August, and the forthcoming Beer Belly Blowout promised to be a nudge more entertaining than a railroad disaster.

"Soup," I asked, "what do we need a whole bunch of shoes for?"

"Oh, you'll see."

Sorting through another heap of rubbish, I knew it was futile to keep pressing Soup Vinson to tell me exactly what we were doing, or why we were doing it. Bending down, I uncovered something. It was an old black shoe.

"Soup, I found one."

"So did I," he hollered back. "Does yours have a good thick sole on the bottom?"

As I turned it over, one quick look informed me that Soup might be disappointed. "No," I said. "In fact, it doesn't have a sole at all. Do you still want to save it?"

"Nope. Keep searching."

We searched.

It took me at least one wasted hour, but I finally stumbled onto what it was Soup was seeking. An entire box of old shoes. I yelled at him to come and look. Bounding my way, leaping over hurdles of trash, his entire body radiated enthusiasm. But then his face shattered into shards of disappointment.

"Rob, those are shoes for *ladies*."

"So what?"

"The heels are too high. What we can use best are *flat* shoes, the kind *men* wear."

I reached my hand down into the box, felt something, then extracted it. In my grasp was a man's brown work shoe. One with a thick sole.

Soup grinned.

"Perfect," he said. "Rob, you're a whiz."

I looked at the old brown shoe. "What's perfect about it? If you ask me, even some old barefooted hobo wouldn't put his dirty foot in this thing."

Soup shook his head.

"We're not using the *shoes*, Rob. All we'll use is *soles*." Soup held up both hands in a measuring gesture, as though showing me how long a fish was. "I'd say we could use about twenty soles, just to be on the safe side."

Whatever it was Soup Vinson was planning to construct from the soles of twenty old shoes, he was certain keeping it a secret. And a mystery. I knew better than to keep asking. Eventually, I'd discover what his insanity amounted to, when it was probable too late.

Soup and I emptied out the entire box of old shoes. And struck gold! There were male shoes aplenty. But the man who had discarded them had very large feet. His shoes could have possible even fitted the feet of Uncle Virus. As I clearly recalled, Uncle Vi's boots resembled twin coal scuttles, and were almost as big as Janice Riker's.

Together, we pulled all the soles off and stuffed them into Soup's burlap sack.

We still looked for more.

"Yup," said Soup as we continued pawing through mound after mound of stinking debris, "we just might pull a nifty surprise on Janice."

"What's it going to be?"

"Oh, it's a surprise. I dassn't tell you, on account you'd probably spill it all to your mother and to your Aunt Carrie, or possible talk in your sleep. Rob, it'll keep best if you're not overly informed about my plan until the time comes."

"We're *not* going back to Swill's Hole," I said firmly. "We were doggone lucky to get out of that smelly place alive. I keep remembering the person you were standing on. If he wasn't dead, he was certain close to it."

"Maybe," said Soup, "he was only out cold. It's possible the drummer hit him by accident, during his 'Beautiful Dreamer' solo."

After finding a dozen more shoes, Soup decided that we had enough. His sack, which I was now carrying, was starting to weigh heavily on my shoulder, which (if I knew Luther Wesley Vinson) was the sole reason I was assigned the chore of toting our cargo.

"Home we go," said Soup.

Leaving the undiscovered booty of The Dump for future fortunates to salvage, we headed toward Soup's house. To be more specific, to his barn. Nobody was around. Uncle Vi's motorcycle was nowhere to be seen, and Soup's parents were inside the house. We halfway overheard them talking. They were discussing something called Prohibition which was currently in effect, and how something or other was being made illegally, and sold in places such as Swill's.

"No color in it," Mr. Vinson said. "Ya can't tell it from just plain old everyday water."

Into the barn we scurried. And it felt rather relieving to unload myself of the sack of old shoe parts. My shoulder had recently started to ache. Soup opened the bag, dumping all of our precious collection of shoe soles on the barn floor.

"Now," he said, "for the glue."

I stared at him blankly. "Glue?"

Standing among our pile of shoe bottoms, Soup's eyes began to sparkle, as though moved by supernatural forces. Holding his arms straight in the air, fingers extended, Soup seemed to be calling on spirits from on high. "Rob," he said, "this could be our very first religious experience." He looked at me. "Don't you get it?"

"Get what?" I asked him.

"We're *saving soles*."

Eight

My evening chores were done.

After supper, it was still light outside and would be for a good hour, so I ran uproad to Soup's house.

I found Soup outdoors, standing beside a sagging hammock which swayed suspended between two maple trees. Both of the trees were bending, and for good reason, because of the weight in the hammock. It was none other than Soup's large uncle. His motorcycle was attached to his ankle by a long, stout chain.

"Wake up, Uncle Vi," said Soup.

Uncle Vi opened one bloodshot eye, winced, then closed it again. "It's still day," he complained.

"I don't usual do too much in the daytime."

"Why not?" Soup asked him.

"Because," said Uncle Vi, "night is more fun. After dark, you can do a lot more, get away with it, and seldom end up in the slammer." But then he opened his eye again, rather quickly. "Luther," he said to Soup, "you didn't tell your mother about the three of us in Swill's Hole, did you?"

"No," said Soup. "It'll be our secret."

"Good," said Uncle Vi. "If we all kept more secrets, we'd probable have ourselfs a wetter world. By the way, do you guys happen to know what time it is?"

"It's about half past seven," Soup said.

"Thanks." Uncle Vi smiled. "Tonight," he said, "soon as it's dark, I maybe got me a date with Tacky Lugwench." He sighed. "Boy, what a loco-motion. She fills her blue jeans better'n milk fills a bucket. Tacky doesn't walk. She sloshes."

"I hope you have fun, Uncle Vi," said Soup.

"Yeah," I added, "me too."

"Well," he said, "I don't guess I want to take her to Swill's again. In *that* place, there's just a few too many unsavory characters. It's worse'n a court-house. But I can't go to pay a call on Tacky empty-handed. I gotta take 'er some hooch."

"What's hooch?" I asked Uncle Vi.

"Booze." Eyes closed, he made a sorry face. "But it might be tough to dig up a jar in this town."

"What kind of a jar does hooch come in?" Soup asked.

"Oh, you know," said Uncle Vi, "It's the kind of glass jar with a clamp lid, like your mother uses to can stuff away for winter."

Soup and I looked at each other. As we did so, I figured that Soup was also remembering what we had discovered, buried deep beneath the hay inside old Mr. Micah Tightknicker's barn.

"Uncle Vi," asked Soup, "does this particular hooch you're talking about sort of look anything like plain everyday water?"

With his eyes still closed, Uncle Vi nodded. "Yeah," he said. "Hooch looks exactly like water. No color to it at all. Clear as a glass jar." Raising his head an inch or two, Soup's uncle opened one eye. "How come you two rascals know so much about whiskey?"

"We don't," Soup said quickly.

"No," I blurted out, "we don't know the first thing about hooch or even where Mr. Micah Tightknicker hides it."

Uncle Vi opened both eyes.

"Well, now," he said softly in his deep voice, "ain't it interesting that you fellers don't know where the hooch is hid." He tried to sit up. "Tell me, boys, who else around here don't you know?"

"Nobody," said Soup.

"That's certain right," I said. "Nobody in town

knows a doggone thing. Soup and I don't even know *that* much."

Sitting up, Uncle Virus winced, put a hand to his brow as though his head was hurting, and then looked at me. Then at Soup. As his eyes rolled, he sort of studied both of us with the same glance.

"By jingle," said Uncle Vi, "I would just about wager that you youngsters know maybe a bit more than you're telling." He smiled his resplendent metallic smile. "Let's pretend that you know where these water jars really are, and that somebody would pay you little sharpies a *dollar* for every jar you could find."

I swallowed. "A whole dollar?"

Soup asked, "For every single jar?"

Reaching into his wallet, which was chained to his belt, Uncle Vi fetched out a dollar bill, with George Washington on it, and let it flutter like a little flag in the August evening breeze. Uncle Vi was now smiling so wide that the stainless steel began to show, behind his lips. But then he straightened his face, closed his mouth, and waved Mr. Washington back and forth. I kept staring at the dollar.

So did Soup.

Then, in a flash, the dollar seemed to disappear back inside the big wallet.

"However," said Uncle Vi, "you little twerps don't know a thing. I forgot. For a minute there, I was starting to imagine that you boys somehow made a discovery. You perhaps found a secret hiding place where Mr. Micah Tightknicker stores his . . . *water.*"

"It's not in the hay barn," I said, feeling more than just a little mite scared.

"No," said Soup, "and it's not under the hay."

"We don't know where it is," I said. "Soup and I haven't seen *one* of those jars, not even one out of a *hundred.*"

Uncle Vi licked his lips. "A hundred jars of water." He whistled a long descending note. "That sure is a pity that neither of you knows where it's hiding."

We shook our heads.

"One thing for certain," said Uncle Vi, "there'd be no sense in searching under the hay in old Micah's barn. So I don't guess I'll bother wasting my time doing such."

I felt my knees knocking. Somewhere, deep down inside my stomach, I was realizing that things were going wrong, and that I didn't want anything bad to happen to Uncle Vi, because I wanted him for *my* uncle too. And now he might be heading for trouble. It felt worse to know that Soup and I might be the chief cause of Uncle Vi's drinking, even though neither of us intended bad luck to anybody. I didn't want Uncle Vi to drink whiskey or to steal it.

With a deep contemplative groan, Uncle Vi sank back into the hammock, closed his eyes, and smiled.

"Boys," he said, "the two of you might run along

and play now, on account your old Uncle Vi's got some serious cogitating to do, before midnight tonight."

"Midnight?" asked Soup.

Uncle Vi nodded. He seemed to be almost asleep, or in a trance. Yet his napping was short lived. Two other members of the Hardboilers arrived on their motorcycles, to see Virus. Their names were Roach and Castor, and I didn't like the way Uncle Vi was whispering to them, and pointing toward town. Soup and I were hiding behind a peony bush, too far away to overhear everything that was said.

Yet enough.

I did hear the word *truck*. And later, Roach and Castor repeated the time, *midnight*. Then they said that this *caper* would be quite a hefty *haul*. Somebody also mumbled another word. *Barn*.

"Rob," said Soup, "I don't like Roach and Castor. They don't act like Uncle Vi."

"They look like crooks to me," I said, "because their faces are so mean."

While we lay hidden behind the peony bush, we saw Roach and Castor walking back to their motorcycles. They coughed up a start, then left. I was happy to see them go.

"Soup," I said, "maybe just this once it won't be you and me in trouble. This time, it's your uncle."

"We'll have to change my plan," Soup said.

"Whatever we do," I told my pal, "we best do it doggone soon, or Uncle Vi could be caught and go to jail. Then he'd never meet *the perfect girl*."

"Right," said Soup. Then he grinned.

"What's so funny?"

"Rob," he said, "it looks to me like we located our added dimension just in the nick of time."

"What added dimension?" I asked.

"Our shoe soles."

Nine

"Rob."

If there was one thing I didn't want to hear, it was my name. Not when I was dreaming so sweet an adventure with Norma Jean Bissell.

In my dream it was Valentine's Day, and my mother had baked me a very special twenty-layer cake, in the shape of a giant heart, topped with globs of pink creamy frosting. Adorning the cake were candles. Dozens of them. Then, as I blew out all of the candles, up and out of the cake popped nobody else but *the perfect girl,* Norma Jean.

In a gown of white with silvery spangles, Norma Jean Bissell seemed to be a combination of Cinderella and Heidi and Snow White, all in one.

"Ah," I said, feeling quite romantic, even though Norma Jean was also wearing a catcher's mitt.

"Rob," said somebody else, and my romance suddenly drained away like cold coffee poured down a sink.

No, I was thinking, *I don't want to wake up. Not now.* Certainly not at a moment when N.J.B. was popping like a tart out of my cake, blowing me kisses, and also whispering my name in a beckoning tone.

"Robert Peck," she was sighing.

"Yes, yes, *yes,*" I responded.

"Rob, wake up," came the foreign voice.

Annoyed, I woke up.

"Rob, it's me."

Kicking my feet out of bed and onto the floor, I somehow went staggering to my bedroom window, to look outside. Below, bathed in moonlight, was not Norma Jean Bissell.

It was Soup.

"Get dressed, Rob," he hissed.

Pouting, I rubbed my eyes. "Why?"

"Because," said Soup, "it's almost close to midnight, in case you somehow have already forgotten."

"Quiet," I whispered. "If you wake up my parents or *Aunt Carrie,* heck won't hold it all. She'll come after the both of us with the old shotgun she keeps under her bed, for prowlers."

"Okay," he said. "Now get dressed."

"Soup, it's the middle of the night. It's time for sleeping, not standing outside somebody's window and spoiling a really nifty dream."

"What dream?" he asked me.

"None of your business," I grumbled.

"I'll bet," he whispered up to my window, "you were dreaming about Norma Jean."

"No," I said.

"See," he said. "That proves it. But never mind about her, because you and I have more important matters to attend to. Adventure awaits."

"Like what?"

"Well," said Soup, "like maybe saving Uncle Vi from making a big mistake, with good old Roach and Castor. So pull on a pair of pants and let's be doing it. And sudden soon."

I sighed. "Okay."

"Hurry."

As I kicked out of my pajama pants, and stepped into a pair of jeans, I began to wonder why I was going to go with Soup, off somewhere in the middle of the night. In a shake, I was out of my bedroom window, across the roof, and down the spreading apple tree which cuddled close to the rear of our farmhouse.

As I hit the ground in my bare feet, I heard Soup's suggestion. "Rob, let's go. We probable don't have much more than a minute to spare."

"Where are we going?"

"To our house."

"Why?"

Soup sighed. "Because, if memory serves me correctly, those two snarling citizens named Roach and Castor are coming to get Uncle Virus with a truck, and they'll be heading for . . . you know where."

"To Mr. Micah Tightknicker's barn."

Soup nodded. "Right. But they'll have to find it first, and that'll give us the extra time we need."

We ran through the night.

Soup was wearing sneakers. So the run we made to his house over the pebbles on the dirt road didn't really bother his feet a whole lot. Yet it sure did mine. By the time we reached Soup's house, I was limping, hopping, and calling him a few fancy terms that I had learned from a long association with Janice Riker.

"Stop your griping," said Soup.

"My feet are killing me," I admitted.

"Good. This'll toughen 'em up."

"Where is your Uncle Vi?"

"He's here. He rode his motorcycle, earlier, to visit Tacky, but then rode home in good season. And whistling."

We hid.

Sure enough, a truck arrived, and it stopped so close to where Soup and I were hiding that I read the truck's rear bumper sticker.

BE CAREFUL IF PASSING.

DRIVER CHEWS TOBACCO.

In the darksome, I could easily identify both Roach and Castor, those two endearing members of the Hardboiler Motorcycle Club. Yet they didn't ride their motorcycles. Instead, they had arrived in a small beat-up pickup truck, collected Uncle Vi, and the three of them chugged down the road, in the direction of town. The truck's motor didn't sound too healthy.

"Okay," said Soup, "now's our chance."

As he raced toward his barn, I followed, wondering what Soup was up to, and why we were stumbling around in the dark at midnight. I soon learned why.

"Now," said Soup, as he produced two glued stacks of old shoe soles, "this'll prove how creativity pays off whenever the chips are down."

"What chips?" I asked Soup.

"Buffalo," he answered, and then grinned. "Now then," he told me, "help me lace my feet into these."

I looked down. At his feet were a strange pair of shoes, but even in the dark, I could see how different they were. I saw a pair of shoes, each with soles about a foot thick, composed of the bottoms of the old shoes we had collected at The Dump. Now, as he suddenly stood, my pal Luther Wesley Vinson was near to a foot taller.

"Why?" I asked him, looking up into his face. "Soup, how come you want to be so doggone tall? You can't walk in those things."

Soup grinned at me. "I don't plan on *walking*."

With his arm, he steadied himself on my shoulder as we made our way toward our target, the one goal which I was dreading.

"No," I said, glancing down at Soup's makeshift shoes, which had heightened him.

"Yes," he insisted.

"You're not going to do it."

"Ah, but I am. And what's more, you're going to come with me. Rob, old sport, you'll be a hero among both men and boys. An epic figure in an era of your own time. Or, in your own mind."

"Swell."

"Rob, old top, be a believer. You're the last individual on earth who would beg for quarter when such a banner moment is about to unfurl. But let's shake a leg. We've got to reach town ahead of those three guys, and doctor the hooch."

With my help, Soup headed straight for the object of my worst fears.

Uncle Vi's motorcycle.

"Originally," said Soup, "my plan was only to take the motorcycle for a fling. But now, we'll have to borrow it for a more important matter." Swinging a leg high, Soup vaulted onto the black saddle, seated himself, then motioned for me to join him.

"Come on, Rob. We can't afford to waste even a second. Opportunity is ticking away. Tick, tick, tick."

"So that's what all those old shoe soles are for," I said, staring down in the dark, noticing how Soup Vinson's feet and legs were now long enough to reach the footrests of the motorcycle.

Dangling from a handlebar was a pair of motorcycle goggles. A very large pair because they belonged to a large person, Uncle Vi.

"If I ride in front," I said, "I ought to wear the goggles."

"Sure," said Soup, "but I have to handle some of the steering. Maybe I should wear them."

As it worked out, we found that if we put our heads together, with Soup's left ear touching my right, *both* of us could wear the goggles. My right eye looked through the left lens, while Soup's left eye stared out through the right lens. It really didn't make too much difference, as the lenses were equally scummy.

"Rob," said Soup, "we've really put our heads together on this one. We're ready to ride, old buckaroo."

Knowing how foolish a move this would probable turn out to be, I held on, in front of Soup. Why I did it I will never understand. Earlier, both Mama and Aunt Carrie had lectured me on the countless perils of motorcycling, although neither lady had

as much as even touched one. Yet here I was,
astride, wondering whether or not Soup could actually do it.

Rising behind me. Soup kick-started the engine
with one downward thrust of his heavily soled foot.

VVRRRUUUMMMM, purred the engine, as the
entire machine was now vibrating beneath me, as
if warning me of its limitless speed and power. As
Soup twisted the fuel handle, the purr became a
powerful roar.

"I want to get off, Soup."

"No you don't. Besides, I can't make it go all by
myself. Rob, you have to shift the gears while I do
half of the steering, control the gas, and work the
suicide clutch. You'll have to steer the other handle, and also squeeze the brake lever. It's right
there below your handle grip."

"Here?"

"That's it." Soup took a deep breath. "Okay, old
sport, here we go. And I'm glad I sent away for that
instruction manual . . . on how to ride a motorcycle."

"Did you read it?" I hopefully asked.

"I will. If it ever arrives."

My body stiffened. "You mean . . ."

I never got the chance to finish my question.
Because right then, Soup gunned the gas, kicked at
the suicide clutch, and we bolted forward faster
than a spooked rabbit. Both of us were steering.
But instead of heading the motorcycle toward
town, we made a sudden and unexpected turn.

"Soup," I hollered, "we're going to run off the road! Watch out."

Beside me, I heard Soup chuckle. "Don't worry," he assured me. "We're not taking the road. We can't let Uncle Vi and Roach and Castor catch us on this thing. It's not ours."

In panic, I was yelling. "Not going on the road? How in the heck'll we get there?"

"We're taking the Short Cut."

Ten

BAM.

When the motorcycle suddenly backfired, two objects crashed inside my head. My eardrums met. Soup, however, was laughing.

"Wow," he said, "this is what I call one heck of a crazy ride."

"Slow down, Soup."

"I can't. Because I have to rev up the motor right before I kick in the clutch so you can shift gears."

"But I don't know how."

"Good golly, Rob. Weren't you watching the other day when we were riding with Uncle Vi?"

"Well . . . sort of."

"Great. Do it."

"Are you clutching?" I asked, with all the hope of a fish flopping inside a fisherman's bucket.

"No," said Soup. "I'm choking."

"Then clutch."

"Okay, now I'm clutching. Shift."

Grabbing the black knob, I pushed it forward one notch, and the motorcycle picked up speed as we sped between two trees and into the entrance of our Short Cut. Our dual steering left a lot to be desired, mostly prayer, and the leaves were whipping against my face from both edges of the narrow path.

"Now," said Soup, "we gotta shift into third."

"That's high gear. It's faster."

"Right. I'm clutching."

Shifting the lever forward again, I felt the engine responding like a wild bronco emerging from a rodeo chute. It was all I could do to steer my half, and wonder why Mr. Harley or Mr. Davidson called it a *suicide clutch*. The probable answer made me feel more than a mite on edge.

WHAM.

The engine backfired again, sending tiny sparks into the night. Needless to say, there were no lights along the Short Cut, so we were riding along in pitch darkness. Leaves, thorns, and twigs continued to whip me in the face, yet I didn't dare to close my one goggled eye. We were moving too fast. Toward suicide.

"Flick on the headlight, Rob."

"How do I do it?"

"There's probable a switch there somewhere.

Feel around and you'll locate it."

I felt around.

Finding a protrusion with my fingertip, I pushed it. Nothing happened. But when I pushed it the opposite way, a beam of light lit up the Short Cut trail in front of us. Squinting, I couldn't believe how rapidly we were tearing along. Spotting a bump, I tried to warn Soup, but too late.

We hit it.

Up into the night we flew, then landed, and I felt the hard motorcycle seat whack me where it hurts the most. The seat seemed to be up inside my throat.

Small nocturnal animals, those that also used the Short Cut as a path, stared directly into our headlight, their eyes burning like hot pennies. A raccoon spotted us, then fled in total panic from our bouncing beam. So did a possum, a fox, and several owls. Wood rats and mice squealed as they went diving from the narrow trail to its bordering underbrush. They all must have known that Soup was steering.

Frantically, I hunted for the brake. Yet I didn't want to release my ever-tightening grip on the handlebar in order to squeeze the brake lever. It was a large piece of metal, and appeared to fit a hand the size of Uncle Vi's, not mine.

"Soup," I said, "ya gotta slow down, or we'll both end up in the cemetery. We can't save Uncle Vi if we're dead."

Soup giggled. "In case we crash," he said, "I'm sure lucky I've got *you* in front of me."

We hit another bump. A bigger one, and we hit it going much faster.

For several seconds, the motorcycle seemed to be suspended in space, as our slanting headlight beam lit up the sky. Then we landed. The rear wheel hit first and we rode along on it for about a hundred feet, our front wheel high in the air. It was like riding a rearing horse.

"Hang on," Soup was yelling in his gleeful yet suicidal voice, "I'm about to give 'er full throttle."

I fought an urge to *throttle* him. Yet I didn't, being too involved with my half of the steering.

It was the shortest Short Cut trip that Soup and I had ever taken, and the least enjoyable, as it seemed to me to be lasting an eternity. Yet finally we emerged from the underbrush path, out across a meadow where sleepy cows stared at us the way only a cow can look at a fool, heading directly toward Mr. Micah Tightknicker's haybarn.

Because the two of us were still wearing one pair of goggles, my vision was somewhat restricted. My eye that wasn't behind a goggle lens was really watering, because of our speed.

"Brake!" hollered Soup.

Finding the brake lever, we squeezed it together, skidding to a gravel-spraying stop with our front wheel one inch from the barn door. The motorcycle, its engine cut, wheezed and sputtered until it idled and then died of boredom.

Blinking, I said, "Are we alive?"

"Of course," Soup told me. "You're forgetting

that I sent away for a motorcycle instruction manual."

Removing the one pair of goggles from Soup's eye and mine, we dismounted, leaving Uncle Vi's enormous Harley-Davidson hawg to lean on its jiffy kickstand, yet still panting.

Into the haybarn we raced.

Soup grabbed a large bucket. "Here ya go, Rob. Fill it up over at that pump while I loosen the lids of all the glass canning jars."

"You want me to fill the bucket?" I asked.

"Yeah, and hurry. We don't have a minute to spare before our three motorcycle friends get here in their truck."

Working the pump handle up and down, I was watching Soup as he used a pair of pliers to loosen the wire clamps on each and every jar. As I struggled toward him, carrying the heavy pail, Soup lifted a jar to his lips, taking a very tiny sip of the colorless liquid, then made a wry face.

"Yuk," he said. "I'd bet you could use this *hooch* stuff to remove rust, kill weeds, and poison rats."

"I'm sure glad," I said, "that none of this rotgut is going down Uncle Vi's gullet."

Soup dumped the whiskey on the concrete driveway which led away from the barn. The colorless liquid ran down the incline in an innocent-looking little riverlet, shining in the moonlight. Maybe, I was thinking, that's why some people called it moonshine.

"Okay," said Soup, "fill the jar with water."

I smiled. "Right."

Soup emptied jar after jar. I refilled each one with nothing except water. After each emptying, the little river of alcohol ran downhill, growing longer and longer. We found more jars under the hay, unclamped their lids, emptied them, filled the jars with water, and replaced the cap.

All during the brief time we were working in the dark of the barn, I kept worrying. What if Uncle Vi and Roach and Castor showed up, and caught Soup and me replacing all the hooch with plain water? To me, Roach and Castor looked about as friendly as a couple of mad crabs.

Pouring water into a jar, I looked nervously out of the barn door, listening for the possible noise of an approaching pickup truck. If those guys caught us, I wondered, what would they do to Soup and me? Thank goodness that Uncle Vi at least would protect us. Yet I couldn't stem my worry.

Nevertheless, we continued our task, converting jar after jar after jar.

"Wow," I whispered to Soup as we worked away in the dark, "that old Mr. Micah Tightknicker really had a hefty business going."

"He sure did," said Soup. "but we ought to be thankful we're not in that business, Rob. I heard my parents talking about it, earlier tonight, when they both were figuring that I was already asleep."

"What did they say?"

"Well," said Soup, "for one thing, making whiskey is against the law. Some guy named Mr. Volstead thought up the whole idea, and named it

Prohibition. I guess it means that whiskey, booze, hooch, and moonshine are all prohibited."

"Against the law. That means old Mr. Micah Tightknicker got rich because he's nothing but a crook."

"Right," said Soup. "So we're actual doing our community a good deed. We deserve a medal."

"Okay by me," I said. "As far as I'm concerned, all of it ought to get dumped on the ground, and then run off to form a little brook."

"I heard my mother say that grain alcohol . . . that's hooch . . . has ruined the lives of a lot of people," Soup said, as he found yet another jar to empty.

A thought struck me.

"Say," I said, "I'll bet this here alcohol is sort of like the stuff Miss Kelly was showing us all about, in our science lesson. Remember that little alcohol lamp? Right then Miss Kelly warned us about how explosive grain alcohol could be."

"And how dangerous," Soup added.

"Well," I said, filling the last empty jar with water, then clamping the lid into place, "I guess your mother can breathe easy now. At least this hooch won't ruin Uncle Vi. It's all running away in a river and under the fence, to somebody else's property."

I hung up the bucket.

"So," said Soup, "let's just hide these jars of water under the hay."

I laughed. "That's all they are now. They're merely little harmless jars of nothing. I can't wait to see the expressions on the faces of Roach and

Castor and Uncle Vi, when they discover it's only water."

I heard a noise. A truck! Sure enough, I recognized its laboring engine. Peeking out of the barn door, toward the road, I spotted a vehicle approaching with its headlights off. The Hardboilers had arrived.

"Here they come," Soup said.

Up a small ladder we scampered, in order to hide in the hayloft, yet see what was about to happen. But as the Hardboilers got out of the truck, I counted two. It was only Castor and Roach!

And no Uncle Vi.

Entering the barn, the two men talked while Soup and I listened from up above their heads. They hunted in the hay for the jars.

"Vi'd better be right," Castor grunted.

"Here they are!" said Roach.

"Good, let's load 'em into the truck," Castor said. "It's okay we dropped Vi off at Swill's Hole. He'll cut a deal with Swill, for a cash profit, and then we'll make the delivery."

"Yeah," said Roach as they loaded the jars carefully into the back bin of the pickup, "but you and me'll keep a few of these jars for ourselfs, and cheat old Vi a few bucks. He'll never know."

They laughed a dirty laugh.

"Yikes," whispered Soup. "I forgot to hide Uncle Vi's motorcycle. It's around the other side of the barn, on the meadow side."

Crossing my fingers, I prayed. Luck was with us, and so was Roach's and Castor's greed. They were too busy being dishonest to notice. Loading the last of the canning jars, the two men started the pickup, then rode away lightlessly into the night, no doubt heading for Swill's.

Soup smiled. "Those rotten guys are in for one heck of a jolting surprise, Rob."

"They sure are," I agreed.

We shook hands, chuckling, and congratulating each another on one more brilliant escapade.

"Yep," I said, "we did it, Soup. We really pulled it off, got here, and made the switch. Now all we have to do is ride the motorcycle back to your house. And nobody'll ever discover that we were ever here."

Yet I was wrong, because somebody *did* know where we were. Somebody who didn't like us.

KA-BOOM. A cherry bomb exploded.

I heard Janice Riker laughing.

Eleven

KA-WHHAAM.

A cherry bomb detonated even closer to where Soup and I were standing, this one between us and Uncle Vi's motorcycle.

"No," said Soup, "it's Janice."

This time, Janice Riker wasn't up in a tree. In fact she was slightly downhill from where we were, beyond the fence on her own property, standing near the Rikers' pigpen, upon a very large barrel. In her hand I saw something glowing. Then it came to me what the little red light really was.

It was a punk.

Janice was using a slow-burning punk stick, instead of matches, to ignite the fuses of her cherry bombs, all of which she would be hurling our way.

"Rob," said Soup, "we've somehow gotta make a quick dash for the motorcycle. We can't leave Uncle Vi's prize possession here. Janice is bound to find out, and wreck it."

"But," I said, "the motorcycle is closer to Janice than we are now. If we get to the cycle, she'll *really bomb us* before we can get on it and then get it going."

Soup agreed. "We got a problem."

"Youse guys," yelled Janice Riker, "ain't going to get away so easy this time. Now I gotcha! If youse run away, I'm going to blow up your motorcycle. Ha. Ha. Ha."

JA-BOOM.

A third cherry bomb exploded even closer and though I had my hands covering my ears, my brain just about jumped out of my skull. A loud noise frightens me even more than Janice does. It also frightened several pigs. They started oinking.

"What'll we do, Soup?"

"I'm thinking," he told me. "That's why we can always outsmart old Janice. She may have the cherry bombs and the pigs. But *we* have the brains."

"Right," I said. "So let's think!"

BANG.

As a fourth cherry bomb went off very close to us, thrown by Janice, I was starting to think less and tremble more. For sure, mean old Janice Riker had Soup and me pinned down, and her cherry bombs would keep blasting. Even though she was

slightly downhill from where we were, the fact
that Janice was standing on that giant hogshead
barrel gave her a minor advantage.

Janice lobbed another cherry grenade.

WHANG.

This one was even closer.

"She's getting our range, Rob. We can't just run
away and leave Uncle Vi's motorcycle here. He
loves it too much."

My hands tightened over my ears. "If only we
had some ammunition of our own, Soup. We could
return her fire and get even. Or, better yet, escape
and go home."

The two of us were cowering at the barn door,
squinting out into the darkness, in the direction of
the Riker residence. The Rikers lived slightly
downhill from Mr. Tightknicker's barn. His house
was quite a ways away, however, and Micah was so
old and so deaf he probable had slept through
Janice's entire (pardon the expression) shebang.

Some of our local citizens claimed that Micah
Tightknicker had slept through the Spanish-Amer-
ican War and also through Woodrow Wilson's entire administration. Well, at least through all his
political speeches.

For no reason, I ducked.

Wondering when the next cherry bomb would
explode was almost as painful as hearing it go off. I
couldn't help it. Noise had its own sorry way of
turning me into a quivering ninny.

"As I recall," Soup said, as we peeked around a
vertical door beam, "Miss Kelly once told us, in

school, that there would usual be a way to figure things out. Miss Kelly also stated, rather firmly, that *evil* often destroys itself."

I scratched my ear, thinking.

"If that's true," I said, "Janice Riker ought to be given a *suicide clutch,* for her very own."

Soup snapped his fingers.

"Ah," he said at last, "that's it."

"What's it?"

"Janice's suicide. At this very moment, she might even be clutching it in her hand."

"Soup," I said, "Janice Riker doesn't own a motorcycle. Or ride one. How can Janice have a suicide clutch?"

Looking at me, Soup grinned. I had seen Luther Wesley Vinson smile in just such a fashion on several occasions in the past, an indication that his mental processes were cranking full blast. This usual spelled a tragic disaster.

"We," he said softly, "do indeed have a trick or two, up our proverbial sleeve."

His remark confused me. Soup and I had no bombs to hurl at Janice Riker. She had an arsenal of cherry bombs. We had none. Not a one between us, yet there stood Soup, a miscreant grin starting to spread across his mouth. I'd seen such an expression on Soup's face before, many times, and it always added up to one conclusion.

Trouble.

Then he nodded. "Rob, old sport, you'll never imagine what natural force is about to become our ally. You'd never begin to guess it in a million years."

"Okay," I told Soup, "tell me. I'm really in the mood for a miracle, even if it's only one of *yours.*"

Soup looked at the ground. "Well," he asked, "now do you see it?"

I shrugged.

"No," I admitted, "I sure don't. All I'm seeing is concrete, and a little wet stream. A trickling brook of the hooch you emptied out of all those glass jars."

Placing one hand fraternally on my shoulder, Soup then pointed with the other. "Rob, that little riverlet is flowing because of one reason."

"What's that?"

"Gravity," said Soup. "Look where all that alcohol is flowing. It's running under the fence and onto the Rikers' property. And I'll bet it's formed a rather sizable puddle directly under that big hogshead barrel upon which stands our arch enemy, Janice."

As I looked out into the darkness where my pal was pointing, I began to realize that everything Soup Vinson was saying was correct. It was fate.

We *did* have a weapon.

Hooch!

Before I could snap my fingers in awe of Soup's awesome discovery, that liquid actually does run downhill, Soup was already executing his next military maneuver.

"Janice!" yelled Soup, cupping both hands to his

mouth. "It's us, Soup and Rob. We want to ask you a favor."

Turning to me, leaning casually against the thick wooden frame of the barn door, Soup shot me a wink.

"Oh, yeah?" came Janice's cordial snarl. "I don't do nobody no favors. And I don't do favors for a couple of dirty rats like youse two."

"Please," Soup begged in his fake pleading voice, "ya gotta be our friend, Janice. Whatever ya do, don't try to burn up our little brook." Soup's voice became pleadingly plaintive. "We just made it. Our little river is the only important thing we own."

"Yeah?" Janice repeated. There was a pause while she was thinking it all over.

"Please," hollered Soup, "don't burn our little brook."

I looked at Soup. "Will she do it?"

Soup nodded. "If it's mean, Janice will do it."

Then it happened.

Janice Riker actual did it.

She tossed her burning punk down from the barrel. It landed smack on target, on the stream, which Soup and I knew would serve as a liquid fuse. *Poof!* The alcohol ignited, just as it had during Miss Kelly's science lesson. A low flame raced toward us, uphill, but only briefly. It burned out. However, the flame also went downhill, scooted under the fence, disappearing beneath the big barrel Janice was standing on. And where all the hooch had collected to form a puddle.

A second passed.

KAA-BBLLLOOOOMMMMMMM.

It was the loudest, yet sweetest, explosion that I'd ever heard in my entire life. Instead of a deafening racket, to me, it was music.

I never knew Janice Riker could fly.

Yet fly she did, high in the air as the giant barrel exploded. For a brief but dramatic moment of time, Janice Riker seemed to be hanging in space, arms and legs extended, as though pasted against the darker backdrop of an August sky. Then, with an involuntary triple backward flip, Janice fell. Down, down, down, and then I heard a very definite splash. Janice fell like a wounded vulture. But her flight ended when she crash-landed into the mud of the pigpen.

PLOOOSSHHH.

Right after Janice fell, a large billowing cloud of purple smoke began to rise from the place the barrel once stood. Suspended, it hung in the air at an altitude of twenty feet, burped, and then oozed down into the muddy pigpen with Janice.

I heard Janice say a very dirty word.

But it wasn't *mud*.

Twelve

"Rob," said Soup, "we're final here."

Hard to believe though it was, our special day had at last arrived, so here we stood, enraptured, drenching ourselves in culture, attending the one social milestone of the entire summer.

The heralded Beer Belly Blowout.

It was, we both knew, a one-day event which was being held on the infield of Terwilliger's Race Track, a dirt oval infrequently used for harness racing. Trotters and pacers. It featured a grandstand behind which ran two rows of box stables used only during the horse-racing season.

There was also a refreshment tent located near the stables in order to serve all the flies.

Because my pal and I couldn't afford tickets to sit in the grandstand, we positioned ourselves as close to the red dirt track as we were allowed, near to the dusty, noisy action. It had turned out to be a windy day. Dust flew everywhere. On everyone. Yet nobody cared. Amid cheers and catcalls, the sidecar race had just ended. No winner was announced by the loudspeaker, seeing as all of the participants had crashed prior to reaching the finish line.

Earlier, we had watched the mud-fight wrestling, open only to the Leatherettes, and Dimlight had defeated both Pickup and Truck Stop. The burping contest had been won by Natural Gas.

Soup turned to me.

"I'm wondering," he said, "why Uncle Vi hasn't showed up." He looked all around. "He came groaning home really late last night, right after you and I sneaked back with his Harley. And this morning, after chores, I tried to wake him up but he was totally under the covers, head and all, and he wouldn't even budge for breakfast."

"Gosh," I said, "he wouldn't miss seeing the Beer Belly Blowout, would he?"

"No," said Soup, "not on your life. In fact, Uncle Vi was fixing to enter the final contest of the day."

Just as we were giving up finding Uncle Vi, along

he came, on foot, wearing his long white duster coat, pushing his motorcycle, and limping. As he approached us, Uncle Vi's physical condition seemed to be less than prime. Somebody had punched him, a lot, and both of Uncle Vi's eyes were black and an upper lip badly swollen. His face looked like a first waffle, the discolored one that mothers usual toss out.

"What happened?" Soup asked him. "How could you get hurt in one of the motorcycle races? You weren't here."

Uncle Vi gently shook his head. "No," he said. "It was last night. All I did was offer a truckload of . . . *merchandise* . . . to Swill. But then all heck busted loose. Swill accused me of trying to swindle him. He and twenty other guys pounded the day-lights out of Roach and Castor and me." Uncle Vi paused to rub a swollen ear. "Funny thing," he said softly, "but Swill kept saying one word, over and over."

"Which word?" Soup asked his uncle.

"Water," he replied.

Soup and I looked quickly at each other, yet neither of us winked, or blinked.

"Gosh," said Uncle Vi, "I didn't even take one single drink last night. I never knew it'd hurt so much to stay sober." Leaning heavily on his motor-cycle, Uncle Vi took a couple of deep breaths, and moaned.

Soup patted his uncle's beefy shoulder. "Aw," he said, "you'll get used to it, Uncle Vi. Being sober is a lot more fun than being sick, drunk, poor, and beaten up."

Through his blackened eyes, Uncle Vi looked at Soup and me, then spoke. "Speaking of merchandise, have you boys heard the latest news?"

"No," I said. "What happened?"

"Well," said Uncle Vi, as he pushed his motorcycle away from the track to park it beneath the comforting shade of an elm tree, "rumor has it that there was a big disaster last night, about midnight, and old Micah Tightknicker's whiskey still blew up. I heard that the explosion knocked some Riker kid into a pigpen."

Saying nothing, Soup and I merely swallowed.

"The kid wasn't hurt," Uncle Vi added. "But she scared all their pigs so bad they jumped the fence."

Uncle Vi smiled stainlessly.

"Say," he said, "I'm starting to feel a bit better." As he stared at Soup and me, he nodded slowly. "Maybe," he said, "everything'll turn out for the best." Pulling out his thin wallet, he handed a dollar to Soup. "Here, this is for both of you. I'll spring for hot dogs, soda, and ice cream. Go hit the refreshment tent."

"Wow . . . thanks, Uncle Vi," said Soup.

"Yeah," I said. "Thanks a lot."

Soup's face suddenly lost his grin. It just melted off his face. "We can't take the dollar."

Uncle Vi seemed puzzled. "Why not?"

"Last night, Rob and I emptied the hooch out of old Micah's jars and filled them with water." He paused. "Because we like you, Uncle Vi."

"You're our pal," I said. "You said you'd be *my uncle* too." My mother always told me to look for the good in people, and I just knew there was plenty of *good* in Virus Burdock.

Leaning his back against the trunk of the elm, Uncle Vi let out a long pensive sigh. "So you young rascals soured my little deal last night."

Soup nodded. "Yes, we did. And we're glad we did it because in a way Rob and I kept you out of trouble, maybe even out of jail, and kept you sober. We're your *family,* Uncle Vi. Your so-called friends, Roach and Castor and Swill, don't give a hoot about you. But we do."

Uncle Vi started to chuckle. "So," he said, "my two little buddies here merely wanted to save my . . . to save me. From myself."

"Right," said Soup.

As Uncle Vi rested a big paw on Soup's shoulder, then on mine, he told us to keep the dollar, because in a sense Soup and I had earned it. "Besides," said Uncle Vi, "I was going to use my last dollar as my entry fee for today's final event. I was hoping to win some prize money to buy . . ." He stopped for a second or two, to blush. "To buy a ring for Tacky."

"You're not entering?" Soup asked.

Uncle Vi shook his head, sinking slowly until he sat beneath the elm tree, knees up. "I don't guess I'll be able to see well enough for a couple of days." Pulling sunglasses from his shirt pocket, Uncle Vi hid his black eyes from the world. "I just hope that Tacky doesn't see me like this." Again he reached into his pocket, producing a double-thick packet of gum, then handing it to his nephew. "Here," he said. "My teeth hurt too fearsome to chew it."

As I looked at Uncle Vi's mouth, I was curious to learn if his steel teeth ever needed cleaning, so I asked him if he sometimes went to the dentist to have the tartar removed. Uncle Vi told me that tartar had never been his problem. Only tarnish.

"Thanks for the gum," said Soup. "Okay, you hunker down here in the shade and take it lazy. Enjoy a nap. Rob and I'll go waste your dollar on hot dogs, ice cream, and soda. As you said, we'll *hit the refreshment tent.*"

"Good," said Uncle Vi. "Enjoy the day."

Turning away, we left Uncle Vi under the elm tree, hiding from the world behind dark glasses, and perhaps wondering how he could ever afford to buy a ring for Tacky.

I followed Soup.

At first, I figured that Soup Vinson would be fixing to visit the refreshment tent, or so it seemed. Yet I was wrong. Even though he stopped to stare at it, then down at the rumpled dollar bill, Soup's jaw seemed set in an expression of granitelike determination.

He turned to face me.

"Rob," he said, "how badly do you want ice cream, a hot dog, or some root beer?"

"How come you're asking me?"

"Well," he said, "half of Uncle Vi's dollar is rightfully yours. But, considering the present situation, we might be able to spend it in a more charitable way. We can really do something wonderful for somebody, instead of selfishly blowing the money on ourselves."

"I don't get what you're saying, Soup."

"It's like this," he said. "If you'll agree, instead of hitting the refreshment tent, we'll take this dollar to the entry booth, and enter Uncle Vi's name in the last event of the day, whatever it is."

"But he can't win," I said.

A gleam began to shine in Soup's eyes. "Now," he said, "let's not be too hasty. It just so happens that there's a chance, although possible slim, that the proud name of Virus Burdock could be listed among today's company of lucky winners."

"How?" I asked.

Before responding, my pal thoughtfully began to unwrap all *ten* sticks of chewing gum that his uncle had given us. I presumed that Soup was fixing to share the gum. Yet he didn't. Soup put all ten sticks of gum in *his* mouth. Then, as he started to munch, he held up the ten empty wrappers.

"Rob," he said, "open your mouth. Please, old sport, because it could be important."

"Why?" I asked in a hostile tone. "*You* took all the doggone gum for yourself. All ten sticks."

"Never mind that," said Soup. "Because it's all part of my master plan."

"I don't want your master plan. What I wanted was half of the chewing gum, or even a stick, but you just hogged it all."

Soup sighed. "Rob, old sport, you're failing to see the big picture. Here, be the good fellow you are and open your mouth. Because I've got a nifty surprise for you, that is if you want the account of your bravery to somehow reach the eager ears of Norma Jean Bissell."

Sighing, I opened my mouth.

One by each, Soup carefully stuffed *ten* white gum papers in my cheeks, and then ten silver inner gum wraps in the front of my mouth, tucking the edges between my lips and teeth. As I wondered why in the name of heck Soup was attempting to stuff paper in my mouth, I asked him, "Whug ah yoom trigging to doom?"

Stepping a pace backward, Soup studied my mouth for a full second. "Now," he said, "give the Beer Belly Blowout crowd a big wide silvery grin of a winner."

"Whum frr?" I asked, as all I was winning was a subtle taste of gum powder.

"That's it, Rob . . . shiny and metallic."

I forced a reluctant smile. Even though, instead of Wrigley Spearmint, I began to taste a different flavor. Trouble. Bending down, Soup grabbed some rich Vermont topsoil, mostly mud, and then smudged it on my face.

"Rob old sport," he said, staring at my face, "you'll never believe how much you're commencing to look like somebody."

"Humdo I glooklike?"

"Uncle Vi."

Thirteen

"Okay," said Soup. "Now *push.*"

Seeing as Uncle Vi was still asleep, Soup and I quietly and carefully pushed his big black Harley-Davidson hawg away from the shade of the elm tree.

"All we do, Rob, is figure out how we'll ride it to win the final event of the day. Uncle Vi can't do it. So somebody's got to serve as his substitute."

As we rounded a corner, it all slowly began to dawn on me what good old Luther Wesley Vinson had in mind. I stopped, and almost spat out the gum wrappers, because it was a lead-pipe cinch what my pal Soup was possible intending. So I clearly voiced my objection in words which no one could ignore.

"Yud kmnt rud a mdrciggle ona trmk, yd krzee mut."

"Who needs a track," Soup said. "We don't. Please wait here. I forgot some stuff."

He left, then returned inside of a minute, carrying Uncle Vi's black leather jacket, a long duster coat, and both of his uncle's boots.

"Wggss ull thamt stumf frr?"

"You'll see what it's for. It's to help Uncle Vi win the prize money so he can obtain a ring for Tacky." Soup grinned at me. "By the way, I think I spotted Norma Jean Bissell. Wait until she spots *you* in this official Hardboiler jacket."

"Nma Jn Bgzzl?"

"Right," said Soup. "Here, try it on for size."

Like an idiot, I tried it on. As I was doing it, Soup was busily producing a few extra items that he had borrowed from Uncle Vi, pulling them from a big black boot. Out came black goggles, black gloves, and a motorcycle racing hat, complete with mud-guard earflaps. Soup had put the soft helmet on my head. Yet it was hardly a perfect fit.

"Wow," he said, "will Norma Jean Bissell ever be impressed when she gets an eyeful of Rob Peck as a Hardboiler."

In spite of my better judgment, my chest swelled an inch or two (to match my puffed-out cheeks) and I was wishing there was a mirror handy. There wasn't. Yet the thought of our riding Uncle Vi's motorcycle in some sort of a *race*, against a bunch of husky mean-looking punks, didn't quite appeal to my animal instincts of survival.

"Ahwee gungta ruddit ina rash?"

As he smiled, Soup shook his head. "No, of course not. It wouldn't make sense for you and me to enter a *race* against that rat pack of Hardboilers. Besides, the races are all over. When I paid Uncle Vi's dollar it was to enter his name into something like . . . an exhibition. Yet there's a prize. But I promise you *it isn't a race.*"

I sighed with relief. "Gmmd."

"So, whatever you do, Rob, keep that gum paper in your mouth," said Soup, his own mouth enjoying ten sticks of chewing delight.

A thought hit me. We hadn't brought the old shoes that Soup had glued together from the two stacks of soles we'd discovered at The Dump. So I asked Soup about them.

"Whgga blout schloozze?"

Soup winked.

"We won't need 'em. Instead, we now have the real McCoy." He held up Uncle Vi's boots. "It'll work, Rob. It's all rather clear in my mind."

Together we pushed the motorcycle farther and farther away from Uncle Vi, yet closer to the far end of the oval racetrack. I felt hungry and thirsty. A pity, I was thinking, that we weren't going to hit the refreshment tent. But that was located at the opposite end of the track's infield.

"Look," said Soup, "there's Norma Jean and her father, Mr. Bissell. They're sitting up in the grandstand right near Miss Kelly and our school nurse, Miss Boland."

Soup waved.

They all waved back, and then asked Soup where I was. "Oh, Rob's around." He pointed at me. "This guy here is my uncle . . . from out of town."

I winced.

Yet, seeing as the summer breeze was starting to kick up so much dust, nobody could see too well, especially those without goggles. Add to that the fact that the Bissells, Miss Kelly, and Miss Boland didn't know Soup's uncle. And, for the moment, I certain wasn't looking anything at all like me.

Rounding a corner by the horse stables, we were soon out of sight from most of the spectators.

"Now," said Soup, "let's try all of it on . . . to see if you can pull it off." Yanking on his uncle's boots, Soup sat on the motorcycle seat, but his legs still weren't long enough to reach the footrests. "It's no use," he said. Sliding off the seat, he searched through one of the cycle's saddlebags until he located a wrench. "Ah," he said. Without another word, he removed the big black seat, put the black leather jacket on himself, straddled the bike behind the gas tank, reached the clutch and starter with both boots, looked at me, and grinned. His body was exactly where the seat had been.

"I'm your saddle," he said. "All you'll do is sit on my back and steer. The long duster coat will cover both of us. From a distance, and moving, I'll look like a saddle seat and you'll look like Uncle Vi."

"Ah yoom shrittle vrrk?"

"Yes, it'll work. Rob, you wear the goggles and we'll stuff our shirts up into the helmet so's it'll fit your head, and you'll look more like my uncle than *he* does."

Removing my shirt, I was still harboring a pestering doubt about what the two of us were about to attempt, so I asked Soup my nagging question.

"Uzzit a rash?"

"No," he said, *"it's not a race."*

Five minutes later, we were moving along in some sort of a line of motorcycles. The wind had really whipped up and dust was flying all over everything and everybody. All engines, except for ours, were already growling in anticipation of something. I wondered what. And then the loudspeaker called out names of the contestants in front of us, and one by one, off they roared . . . into dust and beyond my goggled vision. As each biker left us, the crowd cheered.

"Don't worry," said Soup. "All you do is sit on me as I lean forward. I'll work the clutch, the gas, and shift the gears."

"Hool wrrkk th bmrak?"

"We won't need a brake."

"The last contestant for this event is . . . Virus Burdock," the booming electronic voice sounded. "As you folks all recall, Vi won the Ramp Jump a year ago."

Just as Soup kick-started our engine, something the announcer had said seemed to be still ringing in my ears, despite our engine noise. Two words were now rattling around inside my brain (in the fear-worry-panic section) like two pebbles in a tin can.

Ramp Jump!

"Here we go," said Soup. "Steer."

As he gunned the gas, and kicked out the suicide clutch, my neck snapped like a bullwhip and I near to swallowed half of my gum wrappers. Forward we sped, yet much faster when Soup shifted into second gear. Ahead, I saw nothing but dust. Well, at least it wasn't a *race.* Soup had promised me his ironclad vow.

Faster we rode.

We seemed to have suddenly inherited a favorable tail wind. I heard the crowd yelling, our engine roaring, and my heart pounding. My fingers tightened on the handle grips. All I had to do was steer. But steer at what? To where? Along which route?

Faster . . . faster . . . faster. Air was filling my long duster coat to nearly Uncle Vi's size.

My brain was screaming two futile words of warning. *Ramp,* and *Jump.* A ramp jump? Ramp jump ramp jump ramp jump. Yikes! We were actually going to leap off a . . . Soup and his insane ideas. I should have known better. An idiot could have guessed.

A ramp jump!

"Yahoo," yelled Soup from below me, inside Uncle Vi's black jacket, pretending he was a motorcycle seat. And we were headed for a . . . for a . . .

"Rmp Jlmmp!" I screamed.

We took off.

Up, up, up we soared . . . our engine grinding and our wheels spinning, high in the dusty air and into the atmosphere above Vermont. And I couldn't even throw up because my entire head had been stuffed full of Wrigley Spearmint wrappers. Yet all I could taste was tinfoil. Below us, I thought I spotted New Hampshire and parts of Maine, gowned in August green. Maybe it was Canada.

"Wow," I heard my crazy pal yelling, "I think we just might *win.*"

Win?

The only prize we'd get, I was now convinced as we roared through the air, was a tombstone. We'd be lucky if we came down anywhere within the boundaries of North America.

As I closed my eyes behind my goggles, I was praying about as fast as we were moving, preparing to die. How, I was wondering, had Soup Vinson ever talked me into this? Ahead and below, something seemed to be rising to greet us. It oddly looked a bit like land. It was big and brown. Eyes closed, I muttered a fervent farewell to Mama, Papa, Aunt Carrie, my dog, our mule and pigs, and to Norma Jean Bissell, all of whom I hoped would weepingly attend my funeral. And I couldn't wait to attend Soup's.

"Smile," I heard Soup hollering. "We're just about to make one heck of a landing. At last we're going to *hit it* !"

"Htt whapmt?" I tried to ask.

"The refreshment tent."

Fourteen

"Dearly beloved," said Gutterball.

As she said those two endearing words which traditionally kick-start a wedding, before her stood Uncle Vi, and at his side, Tacky. All of the Hardboilers and Leatherettes were present, as well as some local people, "gathered to enjoin two bikers (as Gutterball phrased it) into holy headlock."

The patio garden (an alley) of Swill's Hole had been decorated in festive, yet quiet, taste. Instead of chairs, the congregation was escorted to diesel drums, some of which were even partly grease free. An altar, composed of stacks of empty booze cases and truck tires, had been festooned with flowers and garlands of greenery, mostly golden-rod and ragweed, all of which wilted in the heat. Ushers, armed with ax handles, kept order.

Swill, who reluctantly had decided to let bygones be bygones, had stumbled unsteadily down the aisle with Tacky on his arm (abetting his locomotion) in order to give the bride away.

I overheard one of the Hardboilers commenting on how hard to believe it was that Swill McEnroe would give away anything . . . even Tacky.

Music, if one could summon the charity to call it that, was supplied free of charge (it wasn't worth a penny more) by Swill's Melody Bashers, so often featured during Happy Hour whenever Swill's boundless generosity offered two drinks for five bucks, three for ten. The band had mercilessly struggled through a trio of sentimental favorites:

"Who's Sorry Now?"
"Just One of Those Things."
"You Can't Be True, Dear."

"Rob," said Soup, "it's all working out for the best. Yesterday, you and I somehow won the Ramp Jump, yet everybody thought we were Uncle Vi."

"Yeah," I said, "because of all that dust. And then when we hit the refreshment tent, nobody got hurt. We were so covered with food that no one recognized us, and we got away clean. Or rather dirty. We had ice cream all over us which we managed to lick up. Mine was delicious, mostly strawberry. What was yours?"

"Mustard," said Soup. But then he grinned. "The important thing was that we won a few nest-egg dollars of prize money to grubstake Uncle Vi, so he could marry *the perfect girl* and settle down to a sensible life. This'll certain please my mother."

Looking at Mrs. Vinson, I could tell how happy she was, because she was crying.

Gutterball, resplendent in black-and-white clerical vinyl and slightly resembling a police car (her helmet was a flashing red light, complete with siren) wasn't exactly an ordained member of the clergy. Yet, years ago, she'd once done a stretch as a nun, for almost two weeks at Saint Bingo's Convent, so she knew much of the matrimonial liturgical lingo by heart. Someone said that Gutterball had to drop out of Divinity School because she'd run out of mascara.

Several of the Leatherettes, serving as bridesmaids, agreed that Uncle Vi would probable make Tacky an adequate first husband.

Tacky looked, well, genteel enough to merit her name. Mink eyebrows, hair elegantly sectioned off into squares and wrapped around sparkplugs that continually sparked, plus a new inscription studded on the back of her black Leatherette jacket.

EAT MY DUST

The ritual, intoned by Gutterball, was traditional and conservative. "Something olden, something rude. Something stolen, something crude." Several of the Hardboilers were blinking, honking into their hankies, or brushing away a tear.

"Okay," said Gutterball, "listen up. If anybody at this here dump knows a reason, or rumor, why this guy and this chick shouldn't get hitched, let him speak now, or forever . . . if you're packing a rod . . . hold his piece."

Two of the Hardboilers in the front pew began to chuckle, sharing in whispers some private joke. But then Uncle Vi knocked their heads together and they became still, lying reverently in repose for the remainder of the service.

Uncle Vi's sister, Mrs. Vinson, valiantly resisted fainting and was offered a special seat, high up, on a Dumpster.

"So," said Gutterball, "are youse two pigs about to maybe plight into your trough? I fergit exact how it goes."

Uncle Vi and Tacky looked tenderly into one another's eyes, nodding, and plighting.

"I dig you," he said, "baby."

"And," Tacky responded, "I dig you, big guy . . . providing you switch off the hooch, shave, get a job, wash, swear off on the cussing, and wear a fresh shirt at least once a week."

"Yeah," said Uncle Vi, "all that stuff."

"Then" said Tacky, "I really dig you."

"Y'see," said Gutterball as she was raising both her hands in a benevolent gesture, "the feeling's nuptial."

"By the way," Tacky whispered to Virus, "when you're my husband, if you ever get the urge for a little extra romance on the side, I'll let you have it."

Uncle Vi's face lit up. "You will?"

Tacky nodded sweetly. "Yes, and when you pick yourself up off the floor, I'll let you have it again."

Uncle Vi also had to promise to lead a more sedate life and to avoid violent situations like Swill's, or Parent-Teacher meetings, and Little League baseball games. The bride, appearing radiantly pleased, clung closely to the groom. All was quiet during the silent meditation. The only thing I heard was Tacky, cracking her gum, or her knuckles.

"Hey," said Gutterball, suddenly severing all devout contact between Heaven and Swill's Hole, "we forgot something."

"Like what?" asked Uncle Vi.

"Mechanically speaking, a wedding's supposed to be a ring job," said Gutterball. "So where's the ring already?"

Uncle Vi blushed. "I forgot to git one."

"That's okay," Tacky told him, installing a round brass gasket, a ring, into Uncle Vi's nose. The ring seemed to be only one size smaller than a Hula-Hoop.

Soup sighed. So did I.

This was the first wedding that the two of us had ever attended, and I was hoping that Norma Jean Bissell and I would someday have a ceremony of equal pomp and elegance.

"I now announce youse"—Gutterball paused to spit—"fused together like a couple of corroded battery terminals. Or, to get real formal about it, louse and spouse." She blinked back a sob. "Virus, you may tango with the bride." She chuckled. "Everybody else has."

Tacky kneed her.

"Now," said Gutterball, "you both gotta split a pad for the rest of your unnatural lives, or until one of you hits the Big Wipeout."

It was time to burn rubber.

Up the aisle paraded Mr. and Mrs. Virus Burdock, as all the Hardboilers and Leatherettes threw rice at them. Not raw. Cooked.

"So long, Uncle Vi," Soup was saying.

"Good luck to you both," I said.

Swill loudly announced that his bar was now open, to toast Mr. and Mrs. Burdock, and in their honor all drinks would be poured at double the price.

Two motorcycles gassed their engines. Uncle Vi's roared. Tacky's purred. Off they rode together, side by side, a Hardboiler and a Leatherette.

"Well," said Soup, "there goes my uncle. You know, Rob, I'm certain glad he final found himself . . . *the perfect girl.*"

"Me too," I told him.

Soup and I watched and waved as the two motorcycles departed westward, into a soft lavender sunset, dotted by clouds which looked like curdling tapioca. Nearby, a meadowlark was fluting errant prawltrillers in a flight of melodic fancy, while pastoral buttercups freckled the awnless August brome. A wafting hint of bovine manure seasoned the air and all of Vermont lay rapturously in the bower of love.

To the west, a three-quarter moon hung in the sky, an incomplete wafer, like the last crumbling cracker from a Ritz box. A nightingale soon would warble as a lute of eventide. Uncle Vi would be gazing at Tacky, the pudding of his feast.

Smiling his joy with stainless steel.

Robert Newton Peck is the author of forty-four books. *Soup's Uncle* is the tenth adventure about Soup and Rob, who also star in Peck's ABC-TV Specials. Robert Newton Peck won the 1982 Mark Twain Award and enjoys visiting schools, colleges, educational conventions, and writers' conferences to lecture on both fiction and poetry, and to play ragtime piano.

Young readers who write to Robert Newton Peck should know that letters that receive quick answers are those with a *school address,* and not a home address. Please include the name of a teacher and a librarian.

Robert Newton Peck
500 Sweetwater Club Circle
Longwood, FL 32779

Robert Newton Peck on Old Soup